CATNIP CANTRIPS

SARA CHRISTENE

CHAPTER ONE

"It's not out here," I groaned, well aware that my resistance was futile.

Luna marched down the hiking path ahead of me with redwoods looming tall on either side. We had a rare sunny day, and my sister was determined to use it.

Luna tossed her auburn braid over her shoulder as she glanced back at me. "That dark magic is out here somewhere. We can't just wait around for it to find you alone again."

"But is it really necessary to seek it out here?" Callie asked from behind me.

I looked down at my hiking boots as my sisters began to argue. Honestly, I was with Callie. I knew the dark magic would come for me again eventually, but confronting it out in the woods seemed like a bad idea.

There was no telling that to Luna though. She

wanted me to face my fears, so I zipped up my black down coat against the chilly morning air and kept walking.

"Meow," Spooky intoned at my side.

We all stopped and looked down at him, wondering if his meow was a warning.

Callie hugged her yellow parka tightly around her as her light brown eyes darted around the surrounding forest. "What's wrong with the cat?"

I watched Spooky sit down on the hard-packed mud, then he started licking one black paw.

"I think he's just tired. He hasn't given me any warnings since we've been out here." I pulled my cell phone out of my back pocket to check the time. "It's nearly eleven. I need to get to the cafe."

I lifted my phone in the air, searching for better service in case Evie had tried to get a hold of me. She was scheduled to work until one, but she had a young daughter. Sometimes things came up.

Callie looked over my shoulder at the phone. "Let's finish the loop, you'll get service back before the end."

I put my phone back in my pocket, then picked Spooky up to follow Luna further down the trail. We had chosen a hiking loop halfway between my mom's house and Twilight Hollow. It wasn't anywhere near the last places I had seen the dark magic, but we had already searched those areas high and low. My mom suspected the magic was rooted somewhere in the forest, we just had to find the right place and maybe we could figure out what it was and what it wanted.

I watched the surrounding woods as we walked, but nothing moved except for the occasional bird or squirrel. The right side of the trail began to taper off, gradually turning into a steep ledge. On our left the side of the mountain climbed upward.

I moved a little further from the edge, glancing down into the trees below, then stopped walking. There was something bright orange down there, maybe a jacket.

Not paying attention, Callie bumped into my shoulder. "Geez, warn me if you're going to stop in the middle of the trail." She tossed her strawberry blonde curls behind her back, searching for what has stopped me. Her eyes widened as she spotted the jacket. "Is that—"

Luna marched back toward us. "What are you two —" She spotted the bright orange. "Oh."

We all stared, because it wasn't just a jacket. There was a person inside of it, and judging by the bend in her neck, she was no longer amongst the living.

Callie moved a little closer to me. "Should one of us go down there? And by one of us, I mean one of you?"

I held Spooky close as a shiver marched up my spine. When I'd found Neil Howard just a couple weeks prior, I had expected that to be my last dead body for a while. "I don't think there's any helping her at this point." With one arm wrapped around Spooky, I pulled my cell phone back out of my pocket, then exhaled a sigh of relief. Two bars of service.

I selected Logan White from my contacts, then hit send before I realized what I was doing.

He answered on the second ring.

"You know," I said into the phone, "It must say something about you that you're the first person I call when I find a dead body."

"It says I'm a homicide detective," he answered. "What happened? Are you okay? Your sisters?"

Spooky started struggling, so I let him down to the ground. "Sorry, I should have led with that, we're all okay. We were just out on a hike, and it looks like someone fell off the trail. She's pretty far down so it's hard to tell how long she's been there."

"I'll call the paramedics. What trail are you on? Do you think you could send me a pin with the GPS on your phone?"

Glancing at each of my sister's haunted expressions, I explained where we were.

Through the phone I heard a rustling, then a car door shutting. "Send me the pin, and I'll make the call on the way. Just hang tight. If the victim is clearly deceased, there's no reason for you to go climbing down to her."

I stared at the body down the edge of the sharp incline. I wasn't sure I could make it down to her without breaking my neck too, so staying up on the trail seemed like a good idea. "Thanks Logan, we'll wait on the trail."

I hung up, then knelt beside Spooky as he peered over the edge.

"This was just an accident, right?" Callie asked to my back. "Like she slipped and fell off the trail?"

"Or she was pushed," Luna said. "There's no way of knowing."

"*Luna*," Callie hissed. "Don't say that. This is freaky enough as it is."

Luna shrugged. "We were all thinking it, don't blame me for saying it."

At a sudden thought, I straightened, then backed off the trail, further away from the drop. The trail was wide enough to fit two people side by side. The hiker wouldn't have needed to walk close to the edge if she had been on her own, and I didn't see anywhere that hinted the mud had given out beneath her feet.

I scanned the preserved footprints on the trail, but there were too many of them to make sense of, and they included several of ours.

I sighed. "If someone pushed her, we may have muddied up the evidence."

"Now is no time for puns, Adelaide." Callie said, though her eyes scanned the trail. "Let's just step back and try not to make any more footprints until Logan and the paramedics get here."

We all moved a little further off the trail, far back enough that we could no longer see the body down the incline.

With nothing left to do, I hugged my coat tightly around me and waited. I didn't want to think that someone had pushed the poor woman, but the idea plagued me. I also couldn't help but wonder if the dark magic had something to do with it. It had already sent one ghost after me. Here was hoping that it wouldn't send another.

CHAPTER TWO

Forty minutes later, Logan arrived with a uniformed officer and three paramedics. It was the first time I had seen Logan in jeans and hiking boots. Both looked good on him, and the burgundy flannel of his shirt brought out gold tones in his bronze skin. I must have caught him on his day off.

His dark eyes found me as he led the way up the trail. He looked me over, then each of my sisters, assessing the situation. Just three witch sisters and a feline familiar, waiting with a dead body in the woods.

Logan stopped near me and looked over the edge to where I pointed. He stared for a moment, then shook his head and looked toward the officer. "I doubt there's any evidence down there worth preserving, but keep an eye out regardless."

We watched as the paramedics and officer cautiously moved down the steep ledge with a stretcher and plenty of rope. The officer had a camera with him, I assumed for documenting the scene.

Logan turned to me, distracting me from the other men as they reached the body. "We've got to stop meeting like this, Ms. O'Shea."

I gnawed my lip, wondering if he, like my sisters, had wanted me to call him for something *other* than a murder. "I wouldn't mind if this was the last dead body I find for a while."

He raked his fingers through his dark hair—it was a little longer than the last time I'd seen him— then pulled a pen and little notebook out of the front pocket of his heavy flannel. "You know the drill, start from the beginning."

Luna was the one to explain things, though I noticed Logan occasionally glancing at me as she spoke.

"You better not be planning on accusing me of murder again," I said as Luna finished.

He gave me a crooked smile, glancing down at the paramedics now using ropes to haul the stretcher with the body up toward the trail. "If I think you might have pushed her, I'll give you a call, but it was probably just an accident." He looked down toward my feet, then back up. "Do you always hike with your cat?"

I would have said more, but the first of the paramedics reached us to secure the ropes around a tree. Logan knew Spooky was no ordinary cat, did I really need to explain it to him? Or had he blocked out learning that I was a witch?

Whatever the reasons, I wasn't the only one who had failed to call. The last time we had spoken was when I gave my statement against Ike Howard, who had murdered his own son.

Callie picked Spooky up, then shuffled a little closer to me with her eyes on Logan. "Can we go now? We've already been waiting here a while."

Logan stepped aside to make room for us to walk down the trail. "I'll call Addy if I have any more questions, thanks ladies."

"You should call her regardless," I heard Luna whisper as she walked by.

With an embarrassed wave to Logan, I hurried after my sisters, thinking there might soon be another dead body in the woods if they couldn't keep their mouths shut.

I TOOK Callie and Luna home first, then stayed parked on the street to call Evie as they went inside. I quickly told her what happened, then begged for an extra thirty minutes to take a shower and get dressed.

"Another body?" she asked. "I had hoped Neil Howard would be your first and last."

"You and me both, but at least this one seems like an accident. Logan seemed to think so."

"Ooh, Logan?" I could picture her grinning into the phone behind the counter at the cafe.

I rolled my eyes, though of course she couldn't see it. "So is 1:30 okay? I'll be quick."

"Make it 2:30 and bring some more muffins. They were sold out by 8 o'clock this morning. Marcus is home with Sedona today."

I felt a little thrill hearing my muffins had already sold out. I'd only been able to start baking things that were actually edible since Spooky came into my life. It was a strange trait for a familiar to bring out in a witch, but I wasn't questioning it.

"2:30 it is. Thanks Evie."

We hung up, then I put the car into drive and traveled the short distance to my little house. My sisters both lived in the house we'd grown up in, given to them by my mom when she retired to her own childhood home in the woods. I could have stayed there too, but I had always wanted my own place, and running the Toasty Bean had given it to me. I wasn't rich by any means, but I got by on my own, and that was how I liked it.

I parked in the driveway, then climbed out of my little car and headed to the front door with Spooky at my heels. I didn't sense any dark magic. I was always looking around for it these days. After getting possessed by it once, I was terrified of it happening again.

I went inside, locked the door behind me and Spooky, then headed upstairs for a shower. I would make the muffins once I was clean.

It wasn't until I was sopping wet and shutting off the shower that a prickle crept up my spine. I snatched the fluffy white towel I had flung over the shower curtain rod and wrapped it around me, leaving my sopping wet ginger curls to trail water down my back.

I stayed still and listened. The rest of the house was quiet, but I could still sense another presence.

Careful to not make any noise, I slid the shower curtain open, then tiptoed out onto the microfiber rug. I waved the steam away from my face, then stumbled back, barely catching myself on the towel rod.

White mist swirled before me, too dense to be steam. I watched in frozen horror as the mist formed into a woman with shoulder-length hair. She still wore her hiking parka, though it was no longer bright orange. Her entire form was transparent white.

I loosened my death grip on the towel rod and straightened, clutching my towel around me. "What do you want?"

The ghost frowned. In life, I would've guessed she was around sixty, but a fit, lively sixty. The type of sixty year old who would go out hiking alone without worrying about falling. "I'm not sure. I remember seeing you on the hiking trail, then something compelled me to come here."

I tensed, wondering if she had been sent by the dark magic, but there was no green glow nor feeling of malice. "You are aware that you're a ghost, right?" I asked. "This isn't one of those situations where you haven't realized you're dead?"

The ghost looked around my little bathroom as if just

realizing where we were, then turned back to me. "Oh yes, quite dead. I've been dead since yesterday, so I was able to figure that out eventually. What I can't figure out is who pushed me."

I clutched my towel a little tighter. "*Pushed* you?"

She seemed to think about it, then nodded. "Yes, someone definitely pushed me, though I didn't see who it was. I tried to follow that detective, but he couldn't see me." She moved closer, making me realize she was floating just above the tiles instead of walking. "I think maybe *you're* supposed to help me."

I backed away as far as the shower-tub combo would allow, then jumped as my cell phone started buzzing on the counter by the sink. From where I was standing, I could see Luna's name on the screen.

The ghost glanced at the phone, then back to my worried expression. "What's the matter? Expecting bad news?"

I shook my head. Keeping an eye on the ghost, I side-stepped toward the counter, answered the phone, then spoke into the receiver. "Let me guess, you had a vision, and I'm going to be solving another murder."

"I was actually going to say that you were about to be visited by a spirit," Luna's voice replied. "But not a malicious one. I didn't want you to be scared."

I sighed. "Yep, she's already here, the ghost of the hiker we found this morning. She says someone pushed her."

"Oh my, you better call Logan."

I scowled. "And tell him what, the victim's ghost is standing in my bathroom telling me she was murdered?"

"That will do. He's the homicide detective, let him take care of it. Now I have a client in thirty minutes, so I have to go. Good luck." She hung up.

I pulled the phone away from my ear and glared at it for a moment before setting it on the counter. I needed to get dressed, make muffins, and get to the cafe. I did *not* need to solve another murder.

The ghost stayed standing near the door, watching me expectantly.

I tugged my towel closed a little tighter. "Meet me downstairs in ten minutes. I can at least hear you out."

She smiled. "I knew you were a good soul." She faded from existence right before my eyes.

I shook my head as I squeezed water from my curls. Someday I might call Logan for something other than murder or the supernatural, but it was not this day.

CHAPTER THREE

The ghost, whose name was Martha, watched me put my freshly mixed pumpkin muffin batter into the oven. Spooky sat on the floor staring at her as she crossed her arms and leaned against the countertop. I had learned that Martha was a gallery owner from Wickenburg who'd come to Twilight Hollow for the weekend to hike with a friend. The friend had canceled, so that's why she had been out hiking alone.

"Are you going to call the detective now?"

I pursed my lips, irritated with hearing the question for the hundredth time. I shut the oven door, then turned and leaned against it. "Aren't ghosts supposed to be patient? You kind of have all of the time in the world."

Her transparent brow lowered. "Well assuming my murderer is still amongst the living, time is of the essence. They could be covering their tracks as we speak."

I took the pins out of my hair and shook out my curls. They fell past the shoulders of my tight navy sweater, which I would never admit I was wearing because Max was supposed to come by the cafe later.

Martha glared daggers at me as I took my time pulling my phone out of my pocket, then called Logan. The call went straight to voicemail, so I left him a message that I needed to talk to him about something important.

I hung up and put my phone back in my pocket. "Happy?"

"Hardly. Give it ten minutes and call him again."

I rolled my eyes. "As soon as the muffins are ready I need to head to work. Logan will call once he gets the message, and I'll tell him that I think you were murdered."

Her eyes narrowed. "There is no *think* about it. I told you I was pushed."

"Yes, but Logan can't see you, so you can't tell him that. Do you really expect me to tell him that I'm being haunted by a ghost who wants her murder solved?"

She blinked at me. It seemed I had finally gotten through to her. "Why can you see me, but not him?"

I shrugged, suddenly uncomfortable. Though my secret had been spilled to Logan, I still wasn't in the habit of sharing. Of course, if I was one of the few who could see Martha, it wasn't like she could go telling everybody. "I'm a witch. Some of us can see ghosts and spirits."

She pushed away from the counter. "A witch who

runs a cafe. You wouldn't happen to be Adelaide, would you?"

It was my turn to narrow my eyes. "Do I know you?"

"My nephew, Blake, has mentioned you a few times," she explained. "He said that Twilight Hollow is home to three witches. I just thought he was being fanciful."

I lifted my brows. "Blake Monroe? Pawnshop Blake? You don't seem old enough to be his aunt."

She lifted her nose proudly. "I would have been seventy-two on Sunday."

I was going to have to have a word with Blake. "Happy birthday I guess. Were you staying with Blake while you were out here?"

"Oh heavens no," she laughed. "I had no desire to sleep on the couch in a tiny bachelor pad. I was staying with my friend Cheryl, the one who canceled on the hike."

I glanced at the oven as the scent of warm pumpkin spice began to waft through the air, then back to Martha. "Aren't you concerned that Cheryl and Blake won't know what happened to you? As far as they know, you just disappeared." I thought about it. "I wonder if either of them filed a police report."

"Well I would hope Cheryl would have gone to the police by now," she scoffed. "Blake wouldn't have noticed my absence yet, but that's what I have you for. You can tell both Cheryl and Blake what happened, and question them both while you're at it. Only a few people knew I was in town, so they're all suspects."

It took me a moment to process what she had just said. "You think your friend or your nephew might have killed you?"

She shrugged. "I would be shocked to learn it was Blake, but he would stand to inherit my house since I have no children of my own, and his mom passed away a few years ago. And Cheryl has always been a bit jealous of me."

I shook my head, perplexed, then turned to check the muffins. If I thought people might want to murder me, I would do my best to avoid those people, not schedule hikes with them, but I kept my thoughts to myself.

The muffins needed just a few more minutes, so I turned back to Martha. "I'll stop by the pawnshop on my way to work and talk to Blake. Though I'm not going to be able to tell him that you're dead since I should have had no way of identifying you."

"And Cheryl?" she pressed.

I sighed. "Once your body is officially identified, I'll talk to her too. Now I need to gather my things for work."

She glanced around the kitchen. "I suppose I'll just wait here. Or maybe I'll go spy on Cheryl."

"Knock yourself out," I said as I went to fetch my purse from the kitchen table.

I couldn't believe I was getting drawn into another murder investigation that had nothing to do with me, but at least she wasn't being possessed by the dark magic. At least not yet. I should probably stay on Martha's good side, just in case.

. . .

BY THE TIME my muffins were packed up and I was driving down the road, I was running late, so I would have to talk to Blake later. Spooky, a regular fixture at the cafe now, sat in the passenger seat. What had started as a rare sunny day had descended into full gloom mode, making it seem hours later than it actually was.

I found a spot right out front, then hurried into the cafe with my cat and my stacked trays of muffins.

Evie stood behind the counter, talking to Max.

"Sorry I'm late," I panted, hurrying toward them. The rest of the cafe was empty, and the used books on the shelves to one side looked freshly straightened.

"Slow day?" I said to Evie as Max took the muffin trays from me.

"A slow lunchtime, but we were packed this morning," she explained. "Richie had to help me fill orders. You should probably just hire him already." She wiped her hands on her white apron, then started undoing one of the twin braids in her dark hair. "Do you need anything else from me before I go?"

Max had set the muffins on the counter and started placing them in the display case with metal tongs. Over the past few weeks he'd been around almost as much as Richie and the other regulars. Not that I minded.

"You're free to go," I said to Evie. "Thanks for staying late." I walked around the counter, then put my purse behind it.

Evie finished taking out her braids, then fluffed up the tight coils. "I'll see you tomorrow then." She walked around the counter, giving Max a wave, and stopping to pet Spooky on her way out.

Max put the last muffin in the display case, then turned to me. "So another body, huh?"

I smiled. Of course Evie had told him. "Hopefully no one you know this time." I glanced toward the front door as the bell on it jingled.

Logan stepped inside, still in his hiking boots and jeans.

Max looked from Logan, to me. "I thought Evie said it was an accident."

Logan reached us before I could answer. "I saw your car out front and figured I'd return your call in person. What's up?"

I didn't miss Max's frown, but I couldn't exactly explain what was going on to him. "Do you mind waiting for a minute?" I asked him. "There's something I need to speak with the detective about privately."

Max gave me his best charming smile. "I'll wait all day if I can have one of those muffins."

I smirked. "You know you can help yourself."

I looked to Logan, finding that he was the one frowning now, then nodded in the direction of my office.

He followed me back, and to my surprise, Spooky joined us. Usually if Max was around, the cat was in his lap.

Logan shut the door behind us, sealing us in the

small space before I realized Evie had left the extra chair out in the cafe behind the counter. Not wanting to make Logan stand while I sat behind the desk, I settled for leaning my back against the wall.

He eyed the papers scattered across my desk. "It seems you've become pretty close with the veterinarian. Was he upset about his uncle?"

You would know that if you ever came around, I thought. "I think anyone would be upset to learn their uncle is a murderer, but he was glad his cousin's killer was brought to justice."

Logan looked up to meet my waiting gaze. "What was it you wanted to talk to me about?"

I pursed my lips, considering how I should break the news. Luna would say honesty was the best policy, but she wasn't the one being haunted by a dead woman's ghost. "I wanted to say that I don't think that hiker fell on accident. I think someone might have pushed her."

He turned to lean against my desk, and Spooky hopped up beside him, sniffing his sleeve. "Not every death is a murder, Adelaide. There's no need for you to get involved."

My temper flared at his tone. I'm not the most temperamental person, but Logan tended to bring it out in me. "Well this one is a murder, you'll just have to trust me."

He studied me, probably trying to determine if I'd lost my mind. "We'll be questioning her friends and family. It's standard procedure, but it will be difficult to determine whether she was pushed, or whether she fell. Why are you so intent on this?"

I could tell he still wasn't taking me seriously, and I wasn't about to return to Martha's ghost with no progress. I hung my head, draping my curls forward across my cheeks. "Are you really going to make me say it?"

He straightened, taking a step toward me. "Say what, Addy?"

I let out a long sigh. "I'm being haunted by her ghost. She is quite sure that she was pushed, and she wants her murder solved." I looked up to find him staring at me wide-eyed.

"Are you kidding?"

I rolled my eyes. "Her name is Martha. Blake Monroe is her nephew. She was visiting here from Wickenburg, and was staying with her friend Cheryl, who canceled on their hike. I'm surprised Cheryl hasn't reported her friend as missing."

"Her ghost told you all of that?" he asked incredulously.

"Right after she ambushed me getting out of the shower."

He watched me for a moment, considering. "Well I guess there would be no other way for you to know all that information so quickly. She had her wallet on her, so we had already identified her. And we found her car parked in the lot near the trailhead."

My shoulders relaxed. "So you'll treat this like a murder?"

He nodded. "A murder you will be staying out of."

"I am being haunted by her ghost, Logan."

He leaned back against the desk. "I'm assuming she doesn't know who pushed her? Does she have any idea who might want her dead?"

I sucked my teeth. He was taking the news better than I had thought, and didn't seem totally freaked out by the idea of another ghost . . . "Why don't you just come by my place this evening? You can ask questions, and I'll give you her answers. Like a translator."

The corner of his lip ticked up. "I never thought I'd end up questioning a victim about their own murder."

I laughed. "One of the perks of knowing a witch."

"Not the only perk," he said cryptically as he stood. "What time should I come by?"

"Eight should work. That will give me enough time to shoo away the last of the regulars."

He lifted a brow. "Won't your veterinarian friend mind me being in your house so late?"

I scowled. "That's not any of his business, nor is it yours."

He chuckled as he went for the door. "I'll see you at eight then."

I glared at him as he opened the door and walked out with Spooky following at his heels. I widened my eyes at the cat. What a traitor.

Muttering as much under my breath, I followed them out, finding Max seated at the sofa near the front door, and Richie Garcia behind the counter making himself his customary Earl Grey. Both of them watched Logan leave.

I stopped near the counter, put my hands on my hips, and looked Richie up and down.

He had the grace to look abashed, which wasn't the expression you would expect from a nineteen year old in a leather jacket and hair slicked back heavily with gel. "Sorry, Addy, I wasn't sure how long you would be."

I waved him off. "The tea is on the house for helping Evie this morning. Grab yourself a muffin too."

I walked away from the counter toward Max, who looked up at me from his seat on the sofa. "Don't tell me it's another murder."

I sealed my lips tight and looked down at him.

"Why aren't you speaking?" he asked.

I smirked. "You told me not to tell you it was another murder."

"Do you have time to fill me in?"

I sat down beside him. What could I say? That I needed to question Blake Monroe about his aunt's murder? That there was another killer on the loose in Twilight Hollow? That because of a ghost, I was smack dab in the middle of things once again?

I settled in as Richie joined us to hear the details. Spooky hopped onto Max's lap and curled up. It was quite the cozy scene.

The calm before the storm, or something like that.

CHAPTER FOUR

At 7:30 PM I sat on my white sofa sipping peppermint tea while Martha talked my ear off. A fuzzy blanket covered my legs, still clad in jeans and not pajamas since Logan was coming over. Spooky sat on the coffee table, staring at Martha as she spoke about her art gallery. Apparently she co-owned the gallery with her ex-husband, but it was a friendly relationship, and they had one employee named Jackson, a young man with big dreams to open a gallery of his own in Seattle.

I leaned my face over my mug, breathing in the steamy aroma, praying to goddess for patience.

"Are you listening to me?"

I jumped, realizing I hadn't heard anything she'd just said. "Sorry, Martha, but I worked all day and now I'm working overtime to help you out, so please give me a break."

She gave me a ghostly frown, then floated into the

kitchen. Spooky followed her, probably worried she would touch his food dish.

I leaned my head back against the couch, grateful for a moment of silence.

Knock, knock, knock.

"You're early," I muttered, rising to answer the door.

Crisp air scented with dying leaves wafted in through the doorway as I found not Logan, but Luna standing outside.

I crossed my arms and jutted out my hip. "Since when do you knock?"

Luna's thick auburn hair danced around her flushed cheeks in the wind. She lifted the collar of her khaki wool coat to protect her neck. "I always knock, I just don't always wait for you to answer, but I didn't want to scare your ghost."

I stepped aside for her to enter. "Aren't ghosts supposed to be the scary ones?"

She removed her coat as I shut the door behind her. Beneath she wore a navy skirt suit with thick tights, letting me know she had just come from her therapy practice. She often had appointments in the evening to work around her client's schedules. "Your ghost was just murdered, I thought she might be spooked."

I shook my head and followed her as she hung up her coat, then glanced around the living room, searching for the ghost.

"What are you doing here, Luna?"

She stopped searching and turned to me. "Making sure you stay out of trouble, Adelaide."

I furrowed my brow. "What makes you think I'm getting into trouble? I didn't *ask* for the ghost to haunt me."

"Don't play dumb," she chided. "I had another vision. I know the detective will soon be knocking on your door. You were supposed to just call him and let him handle it."

Having a seer in the family was the worst. "Fine, you're right, I am getting myself involved. I can't just banish the ghost when her murderer is on the loose. Logan is coming over to ask her a few questions."

Her brows shot up. "Logan can see ghosts?"

"No, he's going to ask her questions, and I am going to relay her answers."

Her surprise melted into a smile. "He sure trusts you to believe you're getting answers from a ghost he can't see."

I glanced past Luna to see Martha peeking in through the kitchen entryway, her eyes on Luna. "Is she another witch? I remember her from the hiking trail."

Luna whirled on her, clutching a hand to her chest. "You shouldn't sneak up on people like that!"

Martha narrowed her eyes, then floated fully into view. "Forgive me, I was only *murdered* yesterday, I'm still trying to figure out ghost etiquette. I would have revealed myself as soon as you found my body if I had realized you would be able to see me."

I chuckled, glad someone else was taking heat from Martha, rather than me. "Martha, this is Luna." I gestured to my sister as I stepped toward her. "And Luna, Martha." I extended my hand toward the ghost.

Another knock on the door had us all turning our heads.

I looked back to Luna. "Time for you to go."

"But I can help translate too," she said as I gripped her sleeve and started tugging her toward the door.

"One witch is good enough." I grabbed her coat off the wall hook with my free hand and shoved it into her arms, then opened the door, ready to push her out.

Logan stood outside, framed in ambient light from the neighborhood. He looked Luna and I up and down. "Bad time?"

I nudged Luna past him out the door. "Not at all, my sister was just leaving. Come on in."

Luna glared at me from behind Logan as he stepped inside. I gave her a little smile and a wave, then shut the door. I understood her concern, I really didn't want to become a target for a murderer again, but I couldn't just banish Martha and be done with it.

Logan looked around as I locked the door. His eyes went right past Martha, now floating near the sofa. "Is the ghost in here?"

I stepped up next to him. "Right there by the sofa, but it's not unusual that you can't see her."

He turned to me. "But I could see Neil Howard's ghost."

"That ghost was being empowered by dark magic. Most the time mundanes can't see spirits, other than occasional glances out of the corner of their eyes."

Martha crossed her arms. "How frustrating, he really can't see me at all."

"It's normal," I said, then shook my head when Logan looked a question at me. "Sorry, I was speaking to Martha."

He looked to the space Martha occupied, then back to me. "This is too weird."

"If you don't want to do this . . . " I trailed off.

"No." He stepped toward the couch. "Just tell me what to do."

"Take a seat," I suggested, "and I'll make you a cup of tea." I raised an eyebrow at his back as he moved toward one chair, hesitated, then looked at the couch. "Or maybe something stronger would be better?"

He glanced back at me. "Could you just tell me where to sit so I don't invade her personal space?"

Martha chuckled. "Tell him to sit where he pleases, I can move."

"Well look at you being agreeable," I teased.

"What?" Logan asked as Martha gave me a playful glare.

I shook my head. "Sorry, speaking to Martha again. I'll try to address each of you by name from now on. She says to sit wherever you want. She'll move."

With a heavy sigh he sat on the sofa, and I went into the kitchen to start water for tea. Or maybe coffee. It was a little late, but the warm bitter comfort of coffee sounded just right.

Once Logan and I were both seated on the sofa with steaming mugs of coffee and cream, the questioning began. It was awkward at first, but we soon fell into a flow of Logan asking questions, then me translating Martha's answers. Unfortunately, we didn't really learn anything Martha hadn't already told me, except for the contact information for her ex-husband, employee, and Cheryl.

It was 9:30 by the time Logan exhausted every line of questioning. He stood to leave, glancing in the general direction of where I had told him Martha was. "I'll speak to Cheryl first thing in the morning, then I'll question your ex-husband. I may have more questions for you after that."

"Excellent," Martha said. "I'll meet you at Cheryl's so I can tell you if she lies about anything."

I repeated her words to Logan.

He narrowed his eyes.

"What is it?" I asked.

His lips twisted as he watched me for a moment. "I want to keep you off this case, but I can't help but think how helpful it could be for Martha to be a silent part of the conversation with Cheryl. She could help guide my questions to reveal important truths I might not otherwise discover."

I grinned. "Are you saying . . . "

He sighed. "Do you think you could have Evie open the Toasty Bean for you in the morning?"

I tried to hide my delight, but couldn't quite manage. Here I was thinking I didn't really want to be part of another murder investigation, yet the idea of questioning Cheryl had me all of a twitter. "I'll have to get the baking done here first thing, but I'm sure she won't mind swinging by to pick everything up. What time should I be ready by?"

"Cheryl goes into work at the bank at 9:30," Martha interjected, "so it will have to be before that."

I repeated her words.

"I'll pick you up at 7:45," Logan decided. "We'll go over what you can and can't say to Cheryl on the drive." He glanced back in Martha's direction. "Thanks for your time. I am sorry about your . . . loss."

Martha beamed at him, enjoying the attention.

He looked back to me. "And thanks for your time too. Without you, this could have easily been written off as an accident, and a murderer would have gone free."

I walked him to the door, then paused with my hand on the knob, remembering Luna's remark about him easily believing me. "Hey Logan?"

He was a warm presence at my side. "Yes?"

I forced myself to meet his waiting gaze. "Thanks for trusting me." I opened the door.

"You're welcome, and I hope you'll eventually trust me enough to tell me the truth about what you and your sisters were doing out in those woods." He walked outside, then called back. "I'll see you in the morning!"

I shut the door, then turned and leaned my back against it, worried Martha would comment on the exchange. But she was busy telling Spooky about having a real homicide detective on her case. According to her, her murder would surely be solved in no time.

I appreciated her confidence in us, though I couldn't quite share it.

CHAPTER FIVE

I woke up at the ungodly hour of 5 AM the next morning. I needed to get started on the baking if I was going to have everything ready for Evie to pick up by 6:30. She had agreed to open up for me in exchange for having Tuesday off, which was my usual day off. I was glad to give it up. The sooner we solved Martha's murder, the better. I had *not* enjoyed her commenting on every single step of my baking, nor on my pumpkin print pajamas.

I slid a fresh batch of strawberry scones onto a cooling rack, then put the lemon poppyseed muffins into the oven. I took a deep breath of air scented with sweets and baking flour. If I was going to keep up with demand, I might actually have to find a bigger kitchen.

I grabbed my coffee mug from the counter, then looked down to Spooky who was looking up at the scones. "No jumping on the counter," I warned. "I won't have you getting cat hair on anything."

If I didn't know any better, I'd say his golden eyes held a hint of malice.

I smirked. "I'll bake you some more treats soon, I promise."

Martha turned her attention from the window looking out over my small backyard. "Adelaide, you're young and single. You shouldn't spend your free time baking cat treats. You should be making dinner for that handsome detective."

I wrinkled my nose. "You sound just like my sisters."

"Then they are wise women. Take it from me, you think you have all the time in the world, then suddenly your life is over."

I carried my coffee over to the dining room table and sat, looking up at her. "But you were married, and you owned a business, do you really feel like there were other things you should have done?"

Martha's incorporeal features softened, and for a moment I thought she wouldn't speak, then she said, "My husband and I were never in love. We got married because I was pregnant, but soon after I lost the child. I don't think either of us knew what to do after that, so we just stayed together. It wasn't a bad marriage, we were close friends, but we were never in love. Once we divorced, I focused on the gallery. And that was it, that was my entire life. No great romance, no children, no nothing."

I opened my mouth, not sure what I would say, but

she made the decision for me by turning away and floating toward the living room.

Spooky hopped up on the table in front of me.

I gave him a soft smile. "Don't worry, I'm perfectly happy with just you and my cafe."

I stroked his soft fur, then stood to go get dressed while the muffins finished baking. I didn't see Martha anywhere in the living room, nor upstairs when I went to my bedroom. I wished there was something I could do for her loss, but she was dead, there was no going back. The only thing I could do for her now was bring her killer to justice.

ONCE EVIE HAD COME and gone, I waited downstairs in a white cashmere sweater and taupe colored jeans. I had kept a small collection of baked goods to have around for myself and my sisters, and Logan if he wanted one. The strawberry scone before me had become nothing but a pile of crumbs as I waited for Logan. It was now 7:55, and I still hadn't seen Martha again. Hopefully she wasn't bailing on going to Cheryl's.

I had gone so deep into my thoughts that I jumped at a knock on the front door. I stood, then walked through the kitchen and living room to answer it.

Logan waited outside in his customary suit. His dark hair was neatly combed. He looked very big city detective.

"Sorry, I hit a bit of traffic on the way here," he explained. "You ready?"

His mention of traffic made me realize I had no idea where Logan lived. I didn't know much about his life at all outside of his detective work. "Yeah I'm ready, let me just grab my coat. I kept a few baked goods this morning if you want anything."

He followed me inside, watching me as I grabbed my black wool coat, then went into the kitchen to select another pastry for the road. I really needed to start making some actual food, but baking for the cafe had me so busy I didn't feel like I had time for it.

I made sure Spooky had food and water, gave him a goodbye pet, then I was ready to go. Callie would be over soon to keep an eye on things.

At my insistence, Logan selected a lemon poppyseed muffin, and we walked outside together, baked goods wrapped in napkins in hand.

"Is Martha with us?" he asked as we walked down the driveway toward his car.

I shook my head. "I haven't seen her since earlier this morning. Hopefully she'll meet us there."

Logan stopped walking to look at me. "Addy, the only reason you're coming along is to translate for Martha. If she's not going to be there, then you don't need to get involved."

"I didn't say she wasn't going to be there, I just said I hadn't seen her. I'm pretty sure she'll meet us."

"And if she doesn't?"

I gave him a smug smile. "Well you'll just have to take me along anyways, just in case she does."

He rolled his eyes, softening the gesture with a smile. "All right, let's go. It will take around fifteen minutes to get there, and I want plenty of time before Cheryl leaves for work."

We got in the car and started driving, heading east for a while before veering north. Cheryl lived just on the edge of a forest, but not the spooky forests near where my mom lived. It made me wonder why Martha and Cheryl hadn't just planned their hike closer to Cheryl's home. The narrow country road we traveled down was lined with plenty of trailhead markers.

I spotted movement in the woods to the right, then grabbed Logan's arm. "Deer!"

He slowed the car as the creature hurtled out of the woods, darting right in front of us across the road.

I watched it go with my jaw hanging open, in awe of its bright magical aura.

Logan had brought the car to a full stop. "What the hell was that?" he breathed.

I turned wide eyes toward him. "You mean that didn't just look like a deer to you?" The creature had resembled a deer in every way, other than the magical aura, which Logan shouldn't have been able to see.

"It looked like a deer, but it glowed."

I stared at him. "You could see it?"

"It was glowing, wasn't it? My eyes weren't playing tricks on me?"

I put a hand on his arm. "Logan, I have kind of a weird question for you. Do you ever . . . *feel* anything when you're around me and my family? I've noticed a few times that you seem a bit perplexed, like when you shook my mother's hand."

He pulled the car off to the side of the road to let an oncoming truck pass, then looked to me. "When I shook your mother's hand, it was like a strange tickling sensation. It happened when I shook Callie's hand too. But I don't feel it all the time, I'm not sure I've ever felt it directly from you."

I thought about it. Most mundanes couldn't sense our magic, but it seemed maybe Logan could. "You felt that sensation because Callie and my mom we're both doing magic on you. They like to read people when they meet them. Luna is more polite, so you wouldn't have sensed it from her, and that type of magic is mostly beyond me."

"So you're saying someone else wouldn't have seen that glowing deer?" he asked.

"They would have seen the deer, they just wouldn't have seen the glow."

He glanced past me toward the woods on our right, almost as if expecting another deer. "So what was it exactly?"

I shrugged. "Beats me, I'm still trying to figure out how you could see it. You might be able to sense a little bit of magic, but you can't see ghosts like Martha. You shouldn't be able to see other spirits either."

He raised his brow. "You're saying it was a spirit?"

"Something like that. Doesn't do us much good to dwell on it though, we'll probably never see it again. We should get to Cheryl's before we run out of time."

He stared at me for a moment, and I wanted more than anything to know what he was thinking, but he didn't speak on the subject further. With a shake of his head, he pulled the car back out onto the road and we continued on.

I spent the rest of the drive deep in my thoughts, wondering if it had been a coincidence that such a deer would jump out right in front of us. We had thought the dark magic was rooted somewhere near my mom's, but maybe it was further north. Powerful magic tended to attract lesser spirits. Where there was one spooky thing, like that deer, there tended to always be something much, much worse.

CHAPTER SIX

Cheryl's home was a massive log cabin situated in the middle of an expansive green grass yard with tall pine trees as a backdrop. We parked on her gravel driveway and both just sat and stared for a minute. The home and its surroundings were nothing short of idyllic.

I shut my hanging jaw. "How does someone who works at a bank afford all of this?"

I whipped around as Martha appeared in the back seat of the car. She gazed past us at the cabin. "Her parents left her this house. I've always loved coming to visit."

Logan watched me staring into the back seat. "I take it Martha has arrived?"

I nodded. "She says Cheryl's parents left her the house." I turned back around and unbuckled my seatbelt. "Let's go see inside. Maybe she'll give us a tour."

"Oh she most certainly will," Martha said as I

stepped out of the car. Suddenly she was floating beside me. "This cabin is her crowning glory, even though she didn't have to do anything but be born to get it."

I frowned and started walking. Martha had claimed Cheryl was the bitter jealous one, but she was making it seem like it was the other way around.

Logan walked around the car and joined me as I left the gravel drive and stepped onto a paved walkway leading up to the house.

"Wait," Martha said suddenly.

I gestured for Logan to stop, then turned to find Martha wringing her hands.

She stared up at the cabin. "Has she been informed yet that I'm dead?"

I repeated her words to Logan.

He shook his head. "I think it's odd that she didn't report you missing. I wanted to see her reaction, so delivery of the news was delayed."

Martha seemed to think it over. "Well, I suppose that's for the best. I should probably see her reaction too."

Logan and I turned back toward the house at the sound of the door opening. The expensive solid oak swung inward, revealing a tall, plump woman around Martha's age, with hair dyed jet black. Her lined skin was tanned deep brown, an unusual sight in the Pacific Northwest.

She looked from Logan, to me, then back again. "I

thought I heard voices. Can I help you? If you're looking for the nature preserve you turned one road too soon."

Logan flashed his badge as we reached the doorway. "Cheryl Isaac? We have a few questions for you."

Her eyes went wide. "Has something happened?"

"May we come in?" Logan countered.

It was an effort not to watch him. I thought I had seen him in cop-mode before, but I'd been wrong. He was totally different when he was questioning someone he thought might actually be a murderer.

Cheryl seemed momentarily stunned, then quickly recovered and stepped back, gesturing for us to come inside.

The home's interior was just as grand as I had imagined. I looked up as I stepped across the threshold, admiring the heavy wooden beams of the ceiling. I could see the living room through the entryway, all done in rich solid tones accented with plaid. There had to be stairs leading up to the second story somewhere, but I couldn't see them.

Cheryl shut the door behind us, then watched us as if unsure what to do, and Logan wasn't helping matters.

He peered around, not saying a word. If he was trying to make Cheryl uncomfortable, it was working.

Her cheeks went red. "Would you like some coffee?"

Martha floated through the closed door. "Oh Cheryl, pull yourself together."

I glanced at Logan, then back to Cheryl. "Coffee would be wonderful, thanks." I hoped we were playing good cop bad cop here, otherwise I wasn't quite sure of Logan's plan.

Cheryl led the way through the sitting room and then to the kitchen. I watched her back, strong for her age, yet seeming somehow fragile. Could she really have followed Martha on her hike, snuck up, and pushed her? I just couldn't see this woman as a murderer.

The carpet was so plush and comfortable beneath my boots I almost regretted leaving it for the tiles of the kitchen, though there was plenty to admire beyond Cheryl's back.

She stepped aside to give me the full view of gleaming appliances and rose-colored marble counter-tops. I didn't see the fridge, but imagined it was hidden behind one of the tall, pristine white cabinets.

Logan let out a low whistle behind me as Cheryl went to fiddle with a coffee pot that probably cost more than my beat-up old car.

He leaned in near my shoulder. "Maybe you should get one of those for the Toasty Bean," he whispered.

I scowled. "My machines are just fine, thank you."

The coffee pot started gurgling, and Cheryl turned to us, wringing her hands. "It should only take a few minutes, now would you care to tell me what this is about?"

Logan pulled out a chair from the dining table to our right. "You might want to sit down, Ms. Isaac. I'm afraid I have some bad news."

She stared at him for a moment, then quietly shuffled over to the chair and sat.

Logan walked around the table and sat across from her, steepling his fingers atop the smooth oak surface.

"I can't wait to see her reaction," Martha whispered behind me.

I jumped, having forgotten she was around.

Logan gave me a warning look, then nodded toward the coffee pot. It seemed I was on the clock.

I headed around the massive marble island toward the coffee pot as Martha went to hover over Logan's shoulder while he told Cheryl the bad news.

I froze in my search for mugs at the sound of sobs, glancing over my shoulder to see Cheryl with her face buried in her hands. Martha seemed shocked that her friend would care so much about her death.

Shaking my head, I opened the next cabinet and found the mugs, then withdrew three of them. I left them on the counter, then went in search of the fridge, finding it on my first try behind one of the larger matching panels.

By the time I had set three mugs, the full coffee carafe, and a glass container of cream on the table, Cheryl had moved onto lamenting letting Martha go on the hike by herself.

"It was just a silly headache," she sobbed. "I could have pulled myself together and gone with her. Then maybe this wouldn't have happened. I thought she got mad at me for canceling and went home. That was something Martha would have done. Maybe if I had reported her missing—"

I pulled out the chair next to her and sat, placing a comforting hand on her shoulder. "It wouldn't have made a difference. She was gone—" I hesitated, unsure of how much information I was allowed to share. "Quickly," I finished.

Cheryl started sobbing louder.

Martha's face was twisted with emotion, and I was betting she wished she could be the one to comfort her friend.

"Can you think of anyone who would want to harm Martha?" Logan asked. If he was moved by her tears, it didn't show. Of course, I was betting he was used to crying suspects.

Cheryl wiped her ruddy face with the back of her hand. "Who can say? Martha was a bit of a spitfire, I'm sure there were people who disliked her. But why would anyone want to kill her? She wasn't wealthy. She and her husband had a clean divorce and were friends. She had no lovers, no children, nothing to kill for."

Martha glared across the table at her friend. "Now there's the Cheryl I know and love."

Logan leaned back in his chair and crossed his arms. "Tell me more about the ex-husband. Are you sure there was no bad blood there? No financial disputes?"

Since no one else had reached for the coffee, I poured myself a mug and added cream. I took a sip and my shoulders relaxed. Cheryl had excellent taste in coffee.

Noticing my movements, she poured herself a cup, then offered the carafe to Logan.

He took it, filled his cup, then left it untouched. "The ex-husband, Ms. Isaac?"

She wrapped both her hands around her warm mug. "Alex and Martha had a wonderful relationship. They were the best of friends."

"Then why did they get divorced?" Logan asked.

Cheryl sighed. "No romance. They were always just meant to be friends."

Martha nodded her approval, though I already knew the story. I gave Logan a subtle nod to let him know Cheryl was speaking the truth.

His eyes flicked to me, then back to Cheryl. "What about their gallery? Was it a successful business?"

"As successful as a quaint little business can be. I suppose things did pick up over the past few years."

Martha's eyes flew wide. "You pompous little rat," she hissed. "We are the fourth most popular gallery in the state."

I was glad Cheryl couldn't hear the curses that followed.

Logan went on to question her about Martha's employee, and about Blake Monroe, but Cheryl didn't divulge anything Martha hadn't already told us.

Eventually Logan ran out of questions and we excused ourselves, thanking Cheryl for her time.

Martha floated beside me as Cheryl led us to the front door, but hesitated in the sitting room.

I stopped and glanced back, wondering what had distracted her.

She was staring at a painting above the fireplace. "That wasn't there before."

I wanted to ask her if she recognized it, but it would have to wait until we were out of Cheryl's presence. As of now, our host was waiting by the open door.

"That's a beautiful painting," I said.

With his back to Cheryl, she couldn't see Logan's narrowed eyes. He was trying to figure out why I was talking about the painting rather than walking out the door with him.

She watched me for a moment with puffy, red-rimmed eyes. "It was a gift."

"From Martha?" I asked. "From her gallery?"

Her jaw fell open a touch. "No, not from Martha. Now if you'll excuse me, I think I need to get ready for work."

"Of course," Logan said, gesturing for me to hurry toward the door.

I did as he asked, with Martha floating right beside me.

Once the three of us were outside the house walking —and floating— toward the gravel drive, I looked to Martha. "Where do you think the painting came from?"

She shrugged her spectral shoulders. "Not from my gallery, unless it was a new piece. Jackson had taken over curating, so I suppose it wouldn't be unusual for me to not recognize it."

I turned to Logan as we reached the car. "Martha says the painting wasn't from her gallery, unless it was something new her employee curated."

"I'll ask the ex husband," he said as we both got into the car. He started the engine, then turned to me, "Though I'll be surprised if it has any relevance. Cheryl would have to be pretty bold to hang a painting somehow connected to her friend's murder so quickly after her death."

"And Cheryl is not bold," Martha added. "Pompous, but not bold."

I kept Martha's words to myself as we started the drive back to town, though one thought plagued me. With friends like Martha and Cheryl, who needed enemies?

CHAPTER SEVEN

I had Logan drop me off at home so I could pick up Spooky and take him with me to the cafe. Plus Callie was there, and I wanted to talk to her about the glowing deer. Even if it didn't have anything to do with the dark magic hunting me, we still needed to figure it out and make sure it wasn't a threat.

Martha had disappeared halfway through the car ride, and now waited near my front door as I stepped out onto the sidewalk.

Logan leaned across his seat, looking up at me from inside the car. "I'll let you know what the ex-husband says so Martha can tell us if there are any lies."

I pressed one hand against the door frame and bent down to look at him. "Or we could both just come with you."

He smirked. "Martha seems pretty sure that he isn't involved. If he says anything that makes me suspicious,

I'll bring you both in, but I don't want to risk it getting around that I'm bringing a civilian in on a murder investigation."

I wrinkled my nose. "I'm hardly a civilian."

"In the eyes of the law you are. You be careful, and let me know what your sisters think about that deer."

I straightened, stepping back so I could still see him. "I'll tell you as soon as you tell me everything Alex has to say." I shut the door, then turned with a wave before he could argue, heading toward Martha up the driveway.

"He's going to question Alex now?" she asked as the sound of Logan's engine retreated in the distance.

I motioned for her to move away from the door. I could have just reached through her, but it seemed rude. "Yes, but next time act more suspicious. He's only not bringing us because you don't think Alex killed you."

"Well he didn't." She crossed her arms and scrunched her face in thought. "Though I wouldn't mind hearing what he has to say about his dearly departed ex-wife." Her form dissipated into white mist, then was gone.

I couldn't say I would miss her. I was ready for a break.

I unlocked the door and walked inside, finding Callie and Spooky both on my white couch.

Callie's strawberry blonde curls sat in a messy bun atop her head, leaving her thin graceful neck bare. Tattoos decorated both arms, fully visible in her black tank top.

She studied my face from across the room. "How did it go?"

I shrugged, tossing my purse on the floor near the door before hanging my coat on a wall hook. "It doesn't seem like Martha's friend is the killer, though she does have a new suspicious painting. Logan is on his way to question the ex-husband." I walked toward the couch and sat beside her.

Spooky moved off of her lap and onto mine, purring contentedly.

"I did see something weird though," I continued. "On our way out a deer ran in front of Logan's car."

Callie stretched her arms over her head and yawned. "Well that's nothing unusual in these parts."

"I don't know why I even try to talk to you," I said playfully. "The deer glowed with magic, and Logan could see it. I think he could feel it when you and mom tried to read him too."

Her eyebrows shot up. "Well that's interesting. Is he maybe not as mundane as we think?"

I shrugged. "To be determined. For now, I'm more worried about that deer. I want to know what it was, and why it was in the woods near Cheryl's house."

I glanced down to find Spooky's golden eyes looking up at me, as if interested in what I had to say.

"Do you have something to add?" I asked.

I received only a continued stare in response. While Spooky had spoken into my mind a few times, the occurrences were few and far between, and usually just when

I was in danger. I wasn't sure what the issue was. Normally if a familiar had the ability to speak into its witch's mind, it would do so regularly.

Callie stood. "No use worrying about it right now. I'll walk you to work."

I stood with Spooky in my arms. She was right, I needed to get to the cafe, but I was still worried. Maybe that deer running out in front of us was just a coincidence.

Or maybe there is no such thing as coincidence.

WE ARRIVED to find the cafe bustling with activity. Evie was busy behind the counter, but most of the chatter was coming from the sofa and matching chairs near the door. Spooky ran for the safety of the bookshelves while Callie and I gently pushed our way through the people crowding around the seating area.

Elmer Brookes noticed me and made room. Though he was tall, in his old age he wasn't overly imposing, but the crowd easily gave him space, almost like magic.

From my new vantage point I could see Sophie, Richie, and another teenage girl I didn't know.

"Tell us again what you saw," a voice in the crowd on my left pressed.

I turned to Elmer as Callie fought for a spot on my other side. "What's going on?" I whispered.

Elmer's eyes seemed to sparkle with excitement. "Sophie saw a glowing squirrel this morning. No one would have believed her, except Maura Wimbledon had glowing robins at her birdfeeder."

I blinked at him, stunned. Maura, the local librarian, was definitely not the type to tell tall tales. And neither was Sophie for that matter.

I turned to Callie as Sophie quietly told the crowd what she'd seen.

The deer? Callie mouthed.

I shrugged, though it was too big of a coincidence to pass off. I'd thought Logan had been able to see the deer because he was something more than mundane, but maybe the deer had been something more than a spirit. Something any mundane could see.

I thanked Elmer for the scoop, then grabbed Callie's arm and tugged her back from the crowd. I glanced at Evie behind the counter, but she seemed to be caught up on orders, so I dragged Callie back toward the office.

Spooky sat in front of the closed door, as if he'd known all along where we would end up.

Once the three of us were alone in the office, I let out a shaky breath and looked to Callie. "What in the name of the goddess is going on? How are mundanes seeing glowing animals?"

She sat on the edge of my desk, crossing her leather jacket clad arms. It was rare to see her honey brown eyes so serious. "Do you think this is related to the dark magic, Addy? Do you think it's messing with you?"

"By sending glowing animals out for everyone to see?" I thought about it, but it didn't make much sense.

Callie pulled her cell phone from her jacket pocket. "We need to call Luna. *And* mom. We have to find the source of these glowing animals."

Spooky watched us silently. I wasn't sure why, but I had a feeling he knew something about what was going on.

I shook my head, casting away my thoughts. "You're right, call them both. We'll all meet at my place after closing time."

Callie stopped mid-scroll on her phone, then looked up. "Do you think this has anything to do with Martha's murder?"

I thought about it, but it just didn't make sense. "I don't see how. She says someone pushed her. That would imply a human, not a glowing animal or the dark magic."

She shrugged. "All I'm saying is that maybe there's more to Martha than what meets the eye. It couldn't hurt to ask."

"I'll ask," I agreed. "Just as soon as she's done spying on her ex-husband."

Callie smirked. "I wonder who I would spy on if I was a ghost. Do you say mean things about me when I'm not around?"

I laughed. "Of course, who else am I going to talk bad about?"

Chuckling to herself, she finished scrolling through her phone screen to start making calls. "If I die first, I'll remember you said that, and I'll haunt you for eternity."

I went for the door. I would help Evie, and leave

Callie to the calls. "Threaten all you like, you'll still be the one that's dead."

I let myself out of the office before she could think of anything else to say, holding the door open long enough for Spooky to follow. The crowd had somewhat dispersed, though most of the tables were filled with excited chatter.

I walked behind the counter to stand beside Evie.

She smiled at me. "Paranormal activity sure is good for business, isn't it?"

I looked at the crowd, noticing occasional glances my way, and realized everyone gathering at my cafe hadn't been a coincidence. I was sure none of them believed I could do actual magic, but they did all think I was a witch, and probably assumed I would have more knowledge of the supernatural than anyone else in town.

They had come here hoping I could grant some insight. Only problem was, I was just as in the dark as everyone else.

CHAPTER EIGHT

Logan called as Spooky and I walked home in the dark. Though the initial excitement had died down, it had been an effort to chase the last few customers out of the cafe.

My icy fingers fumbled my phone out of my pocket, nearly dropping it on the sidewalk. I managed to answer on the third ring. "What did you find out?"

"Well hello to you too," Logan answered. "I was hoping you could play translator again so I could ask Martha a few things about what Alex had to say."

I glanced around the quiet neighborhood, then continued walking with leaves crunching underfoot, debating what to say.

"You still there, Addy?"

"Yeah I'm here." I turned at a stop sign with Spooky trotting ahead of me. "I'm just debating whether or not I should tell you something."

"Spill it."

I glanced around again to make sure no one was listening, then lowered my voice, "That deer wasn't the only glowing animal around, and you're not the only mundane who can see them. Sophie Eddings saw a glowing squirrel today and Maura Wimbledon had glowing birds at her feeder."

I focused on the sound of my boots echoing across the sidewalk while I waited for him to reply. I wasn't sure why I was telling him, but he *had* seen the deer, so it was probably something he should know.

"So this might not be something only pertaining to your world," he answered finally.

"Well it probably is, but it's leaking out everywhere. I've never experienced something like this. I'm used to my world being a complete secret."

I stopped walking at a sudden tingling sensation, then stepped back as a glowing field mouse ran right in front of my boots. Spooky shot off after it, disappearing so quick I didn't have time to react.

"Dammit," I hissed. "Logan, I have to go, Spooky just chased after a glowing mouse."

"I'm already on my way to your house, tell me where you are."

I told him the cross streets and hung up. I would lecture him about thinking he could just show up at my house later, once I found my cat.

"Spooky!" I called out, scanning the darkness. He

had taken off toward a small copse of trees in someone's yard.

I considered the consequences of trespassing for nary a second, then ran in the direction the cat had gone.

My boots barely maintained traction across the slick grass and damp dead leaves as I charged past the trees. I spotted a tiny glowing critter darting away near a fence encircling the next yard, then a larger black blur chasing after it.

"Spooky!" I rasped, changing direction to follow him.

I heard a car screech up and a door opening and shutting, but didn't pause to see if it was Logan. I was close enough to watch as the glowing mouse found a hole in the fence and scurried through. I lunged toward Spooky, but he leapt upward, easily scaling the wooden fence before disappearing on the other side.

"Crap." I wrapped my hands around the top of the fence and tried to pull myself up, but it was too tall, I didn't have the strength. I tried again, scraping the toes of my boots across the wood as I tried to gain purchase.

I lost my hold on the fence and stumbled backward as someone ran up behind me, then turned to find Logan shining a small flashlight my way.

I motioned him closer. "Hurry up and give me a boost!"

He didn't ask questions, he just tossed his flashlight in the grass and moved toward me, then laced his fingers together for me to step on.

With one boot in his hands, I gripped his shoulders

and propelled myself upward, then flung my arms over the top of the fence. The house beyond the yard had a back porch light on, granting me a full view of fresh cut grass and small shrubs.

I didn't see Spooky or the mouse anywhere. My heart fell to my feet as I lowered myself back down from the fence and looked for a way around. Maybe they had made it past the house and out onto the next street.

Logan followed me as I hurried around the perimeter of the fence. "What's going on, Addy?"

"I told you on the phone, Spooky chased after a glowing mouse. They both went into the yard, but now I don't see them anywhere."

I circled the fence, rushed out to the next street, then looked both ways. Nothing.

Logan stopped at my side, glancing around.

Tears welled in my eyes. I should have kept that damn cat on a leash. Now he was out in the streets alone and I didn't know what these weird glowing animals were.

Logan tentatively placed a hand on my shoulder. "He's been around a long time, I'm sure he'll be alright. He'll find his way home."

I wiped the tears from my eyes, refusing to let any fall down my cheeks. I hated crying in front of people. "What if he's not all right? What if the dark magic gets him?"

Logan's hand fell from my shoulder. "Did you encounter it again? Why didn't you tell me?"

I shook my head and started walking back in the direction we'd come. "I haven't seen it, not since that time in the woods. I can't find it anywhere."

He jogged to catch up with me. "I knew you weren't just hiking the other morning. You and your sisters were out looking for it."

"So what if we were." My words came out scornful, though I wasn't mad at Logan. I was mad at myself.

We finished the walk toward his car in silence.

He pulled his keys out of his pocket. "I'll take you home."

"It's only two blocks away," I argued. "I can walk."

"Humor me." He hit the button on his keychain to unlock the door, then opened it for me.

I slipped inside, plopping down with a heavy sigh. I was a failure of a cat mom. It didn't matter that he was a magical familiar. He was still my pet and I was supposed to take care of him.

Logan walked around the car, got into the driver's side, then started the engine. We spent the two minutes it took to reach my house in silence, then parked on the street.

I twisted my lips, not quite ready to get out of the car. I should probably offer an apology for being rude when he was only trying to help, but I couldn't quite muster it. "Martha is probably inside. You can come in and ask her your questions before my mom and sisters get here."

"Sure," he said simply, then opened his door and got out.

I felt sick and shaky as I exited the car, then walked up my driveway beside Logan. I had been hoping I'd find Spooky waiting outside the front door for me, but I didn't see him anywhere.

I unlocked the door and we both went inside. Everything was still and dark, no sign of Martha.

I flipped on the light as Logan shut the door behind us.

"Hello?" I called out.

No answer.

"I wonder where she is," I muttered, leading the way into the kitchen. Things had been so busy at the cafe I hadn't had time to eat.

I noticed Spooky's empty food dish on the floor near the dining table and the tears threatened again, but I held them back. Logan was right. Spooky had been around a long, long time. He knew how to take care of himself, and he would come back to me when he was ready. Or so I kept telling myself.

I turned my back on Logan so he wouldn't see the moisture in my eyes and started looking through the fridge.

I hadn't gone shopping in a while, but there was still leftover pizza that Callie and I had ordered the previous night. While we had never discussed it formally, either Luna or Callie slept over pretty much every night. We didn't know when the dark magic would strike again, and neither of them was willing to let me be alone for it to happen.

I pulled out the pizza box and set it on the counter, then turned to Logan and forced a smile. "Hungry? I'm sure Martha will show up soon."

"Addy—"

I shook my head and held up a hand. "Don't. If I talk about it I'm going to cry, and I don't know you well enough to cry in front of you."

He watched me for a moment, then nodded. "Okay, pizza sounds good."

I plopped the box onto the counter, then moved past him to fetch plates from the cupboard. "So what did you learn from Alex?"

I could feel him watching me as I put the plates beside the pizza box. "Not much. He knew she was coming out to hike this weekend, but claims he didn't know the exact locations or itinerary. I'll have to confirm that with Martha." He hesitated. "You know, I shouldn't be telling you any of this."

I managed a small smile as I turned toward him. "I'll hear it anyways when you question Martha. And I've told you a lot of stuff I'm not supposed to tell anyone either."

He nodded. "True, I never thought police work would lead me to sharing an investigation with a witch."

"I noticed you don't work with a partner," I said, wondering if now would be the time that I would finally get some personal information out of him.

His expression darkened, and I realized I'd hit a nerve. "That's—" A knock at the door interrupted him.

I silently cursed my sisters for their poor timing, then moved to answer the door. "Help yourself to the pizza," I said as I passed Logan.

I hurried through the living room, then answered my door to find both my sisters and my mother outside. They shivered in their autumn coats. Soon the night temperatures would drop enough that we would all be dressed in down parkas.

I stepped aside to let them into the warmth.

My sisters both moved past me and then into the kitchen, quickly noticing Logan and pulling him into conversation.

My mom stayed behind, giving me a knowing look. She removed her stocking cap and shook out her ginger curls, the exact same shade as mine, though now they had a few streaks of white. "You lost the cat, didn't you?"

I put my hands on my hips. "Now how can you possibly know that already?"

She gave me a secretive smile. "Well he's not here." She gestured toward the rest of the house. "I made a simple deduction." She turned away and headed toward the kitchen.

I followed her, grumbling, "Simple deduction my foot."

My mom always seemed to know things we hadn't yet told her, though occasionally we could take her by surprise.

We entered the kitchen to find Logan and my sisters seated at the dining room table. Both of my sisters were eating a slice of cold pizza, but Logan had abstained. I glanced at the box, noticing there were only two small pieces left, and wondered if he had left them both for me intentionally.

Well, either way the gesture wouldn't go to waste. I put both slices on the plate so my sisters couldn't hog anymore, then leaned my butt against the countertop and started eating.

My mom took up the last seat at the table, then addressed Logan, "I fear, Detective White, that we have family matters to discuss. *Private* family matters."

I scowled as I swallowed a bite of pizza. "I invited him here, and he already knows what's going on."

He stood. "I came to question Martha, but if she's not here, I can leave."

My mom gawked at him. "You, a mundane, came to question a ghost?" She turned to me. "Adelaide, just what is going on here?"

So my sisters had told her about Martha, but not that Logan and I were working together to solve her murder. At least they were able to keep *some* secrets. "Mom, he's trying to solve a murder. Don't you think it's helpful for him to hear from the victim? He asks the questions, and I translate."

She stood. "You should have banished that ghost the moment it appeared. Don't you realize how dangerous it is for you to be around spirits?"

I put my hands on my hips. "She came to me for help. I'm not just going to banish her." I sensed a presence behind me and turned to watch Martha materialize near the fridge.

"Maybe you should banish me," she sobbed. "I would have rather not known the truth."

"What truth?" I sighed, giving her a dose of the irritation that was meant for my mom.

She didn't seem to notice my tone. "The truth of who killed me." She looked upward, as if peering into the heavens. "My dear Alex, would you do such a thing?"

My mom approached my side as I watched Martha break down in tears. I wasn't sure what I could do. It wasn't like I could physically comfort her.

My mom leaned in near my shoulder. "Are you sure you want to involve a mundane in all of this?" she whispered.

"He's already involved," I whispered back. "And I need his help to figure out what happened to Martha."

We both watched the sobbing ghost as my sisters explained to Logan what the rest of us were seeing. I was hoping she'd pull it together soon so she could explain what she meant about her ex-husband. Logan didn't seem to think he was the murderer, so why was Martha suddenly so sure?

CHAPTER NINE

We all gathered around the sofa as Martha hovered just above the seat cushion with her head in her hands. "He's selling the gallery," she groaned. "How could he?"

Logan stood near my shoulder. "So let me get this straight, she was there the whole time I was questioning him, then she stayed behind and looked at the paperwork on his desk?"

I shrugged. "I guess it was just lucky that the contract was the paper on top. She's a normal ghost, so she couldn't open any drawers or anything."

Logan stroked his chin. "He just found out she was dead, and that her half of the gallery was left to him. He wouldn't have been able to sell without her agreement while she was still alive."

Martha looked up at us. "So that's it then, isn't it? He might not have been the one who pushed me, but he was involved in my death. He would have never found a buyer so quickly if this wasn't premeditated. And to already have the contracts drawn up?" She buried her head back in her hands.

Logan looked to me. "Did she just say something?"

Callie plopped down in a chair adjacent the sofa. "Only that you guys have found your murderer. Case closed."

Luna shook her head as she sat down on the sofa beside Martha. "We don't know that for sure." She looked up to Logan. "Will you be able to look at that contract? Maybe Martha misread what it was."

My mom moved to stand behind the couch where she could look at all of us. "What about these glowing spirit animals? Isn't that what we're here to talk about?"

Martha lifted her head. "Glowing animals?"

I narrowed my eyes. "You ask like you know something about it."

She nodded. "Cheryl claimed she saw a glowing fox the morning she canceled on our hike. She assumed she was getting a migraine and had hallucinated it. Are you telling me what she saw was real?"

We all stared at her, except for Logan, who was staring at me waiting for an explanation.

My mom sighed. "Alright, *maybe* the murder and the animals are connected."

"What did I miss?" Logan interrupted.

I pinched my brow and shook my head. Now *I* was

the one getting a headache. "Cheryl saw one of the glowing animals too. I think there's only one thing we can do now." I lifted my gaze to find everyone watching me expectantly. I sighed. "We need to capture one of these glowing animals and figure out what it is. We should go tonight, they'll be easier to spot in darkness." *And if I found my cat while I was at it, that would be a bonus.*

Logan leaned against the sofa arm. "And how do you propose we catch one?"

"*You* don't catch one," I said. "You do more research on Martha's ex-husband, or whatever else homicide detectives do. Leave the spirit animal catching to the witches."

Luna leaned back heavily against the couch cushions. "And here I'd actually hoped I'd get a full night's sleep tonight."

My mom stepped around the sofa, her eyes on me. "I won't have you wandering about the woods at night with that dark magic still on the loose. You and Luna will search around your neighborhood. Callie and I will take the woods."

"Why do I have to go to the woods?" Callie whined.

My mom gave her a stern expression. "Because I can protect you out there, and Luna can watch over your sister. Hopefully before the night is through one of us will manage to find something."

"But what will I do?" Martha asked.

"Go with Addy," my mom decided. "You can be an extra set of eyes."

I almost commented that she might scare the animals away, but her face had lit up at the suggestion and I wasn't prepared to take the task away from her. She needed something to distract herself from what she had learned.

"All right," I decided, "I'm going to call Max before it gets too late and see if he has any animal traps."

Logan watched the exchange, seeming to compre-hend that Martha was part of the conversation. "Why do you need traps? I thought you were going to use . . . witch tactics."

Ah, how to explain things to a mundane. "We can try using magic to lure these creatures, but we don't know what they are, so I don't want to depend on magic alone to trap them. They seem to behave like normal animals, so a regular physical trap might be best."

He nodded along, though he still seemed hesitant.

I took my phone out of my pocket. "I'll make the call real quick, hopefully he's still up."

I walked into the kitchen as I scrolled through my contacts for Max's number, wondering what he might think of my request. I didn't even know if he would have traps, but he was a livestock vet as well as a domestic vet, so hopefully he would have something.

I leaned my butt against the counter, waiting for him to answer.

When it got to the sixth ring, I almost hung up, then his voice came over the line. "Addy? What's wrong?"

"Why does something have to be wrong?" I asked innocently.

I could visualize him smiling on the other end of the line. "You've just never called me this late at night before."

"Did I wake you?"

"Another twenty minutes and you might have," he laughed. "What's up?"

"I have an odd request, and I'm hoping you won't ask any questions."

He was silent for a moment. "Well you have my attention."

"I was wondering if you have any animal traps I can borrow for the night."

Another moment of contemplative silence. "Large or small?"

"Both?"

He sighed. "You're trying to catch one of those glowing animals Sophie was talking about, aren't you?"

I winced. "So you heard about those, huh?"

He laughed. "You just can't ignore a good mystery, can you?"

You have no idea, I thought. "Guilty as charged. So can I borrow some traps?"

"On one condition."

"Name it," I said automatically.

"You let me come with you. I'd never forgive myself

if I let you traipse through the woods alone at night, only to get mauled by a bear."

The offer was sweet, and I couldn't quite think of how to argue. I didn't know where else we would get traps at this hour. "Are you sure you're up for it tonight? You did say you were about to go to bed, and I was thinking more about setting the traps on the outskirts of my neighborhood. I should be fine."

"If you really must do it tonight, I can bring the traps by in half an hour. It will go faster if I help you set them."

I thought about it for a moment. I could always have Max help us set the traps, then use magic to lure the animals in after he'd gone home. "I'll see you in thirty minutes then, if you're sure you don't mind."

"What I would mind is being left out of the mystery. See you soon."

"I'll be waiting."

We hung up, and I went back into the living room.

Everyone was seated except for Logan, who leaned against the couch with his arms crossed. "And how do you intend to explain to the vet what you'll do to draw the animals in?"

I wrinkled my nose. "The vet doesn't ask as many questions as the detective. He's willing to help a friend out."

Logan smirked. "All right, at least let me know how it goes."

I gave him a little salute, then moved to walk him to the door while my family and the ghost watched on.

Once Logan had opened the door and stepped outside, he motioned for me to step outside with him.

Assuming he wanted privacy, I stepped out and shut the door. Icy air closed around me like a fist. "Eesh it's cold!" I looked to Logan. "Whatever you need to say, make it quick."

My porch light cast shadows across half of his face as he leaned in near me, his breath fogging the air. "Can you try to ask Martha more about Alex while you're out setting traps? I find it hard to believe that he caused her death so he could sell the gallery. He seemed genuinely distraught over the news."

I wrapped my arms tightly around myself. "Maybe he was just overwhelmed with guilt. Do you think you'll be able to find the contract she mentioned?"

"I'll need a warrant. It might take some time." He looked me up and down. "You be careful tonight."

"I'll have Max and Luna with me. I'll be fine."

"Neither Max or Luna carry a gun." He turned to go. "Call me if you need me."

I watched him walk down the driveway to his car, wondering if he was a bit jealous that Max got to come animal trapping, or if he was just genuinely worried about my safety.

He got in his car and drove away. I shook my head. I had enough mysteries to deal with, I didn't need to add the mystery of Logan White to the list . . . at least not until we'd solved Martha's murder and I had my familiar back.

When my teeth started chattering uncontrollably, I went back inside. I had thirty minutes to change into something warm and prepare for an evening of setting traps.

Here was hoping I wouldn't trap more than I could handle.

CHAPTER TEN

Thirty minutes later, I was dressed in my forest green down parka with a black stocking cap pulled over my ginger curls. Callie and my mom had gone to start searching the woods since my mom had a few traps at her place. She used them to relocate any animals that got a little too bold stealing vegetables from her garden.

Luna lounged on the couch, cozy in my pumpkin orange sweater with her wool coat ready to go on top.

Martha materialized as a knock on the door signaled Max's arrival.

I hurried across the living room and answered it, finding him standing outside with no traps in sight. He looked different with a stocking cap pulled over his normally tousled hair, and a heavy black coat instead of his white lab coat.

His breath fogged the air with his words. "You sure

picked an interesting night to go out setting traps. I think we're about to have our first freeze."

I opened the door wide. "Come in where it's warm." I spotted his vehicle out on the street. "Are the traps in your Jeep?"

He walked inside past me, bringing with him a gust of cool air. "I figured it would be easier if I drove, so we can just leave them in the back until we need them." He spotted Luna sitting on the couch and gave her a wave, then peered around the living room. "Where's Spooky?"

Luna glanced at me, noted my crumbling expression, then explained, "He ran off after a mouse earlier tonight, we're hoping he'll come back soon."

Max turned to me, as if looking for confirmation.

I aimed my gaze downward and shrugged. "I tried to chase after him, but he went over a fence and it was too tall for me to climb."

His hand alit on my shoulder. "We'll look for him tonight."

Martha hovered just behind him. "He's handsome," she whispered, though he couldn't hear her no matter how loud she spoke, "you should go in for a hug, Addy.'

While I didn't go in for a hug, I managed a smile. Max's reaction was a much better reply than, *I'm sure he'll come back.*

"Deal," I replied. "But let's get going. I don't want to keep you up too late."

Luna stood, grinning at Max. "She's much nicer to

you. I haven't heard a single word of concern about me needing to meet my first client at 7 AM."

I rolled my eyes at her. "And I need to start baking for the cafe at 5. Now that we've established we'll all be waking up early, let's get a move on. We're burning moonlight." I opened the door and waited while Max and Luna walked past me outside. Martha floated after them, fortunately keeping her thoughts to herself.

I almost considered leaving the door open in case Spooky came back, but that was just asking for trouble. I locked the door and we walked down the driveway together toward Max's jeep. Luna relinquished the front passenger seat to me without question, a mischievous glint in her eye. If I had a moment alone with her, I'd tell her to stop worrying about my romantic life and focus on the task at hand. The funny thing was, my sisters were both single too, they just didn't have any potential suitors currently for me to pick on in turn.

Max started the engine, then blasted the heat. "Where to first?"

I thought about it. "The neighborhood ends two streets past where I lost Spooky. Let's set a trap there first, maybe we can even catch the glowing mouse he ran off after." I turned toward him. "Do you have any live traps small enough for a mouse?"

He stared at me. "Are you telling me you actually saw one of these glowing animals?"

I tilted my head. "Yes?"

His eyes widened. "So Sophie actually saw one too? I figured her eyes were just playing tricks on her."

"But Maura Wimbledon saw glowing birds," I countered.

"She's getting up there in years."

I blinked at him. "Are you telling me you volunteered to help me set traps this late at night when you didn't even believe what we were trapping was real?"

He gave me a sheepish grin, then shrugged.

I laughed. "Well I've seen the animals too, twice now. So do you believe me?"

He glanced toward the back seat at Luna, then back to me. "Well I'm still not convinced that this isn't an elaborate prank, but I don't think you would make something like this up otherwise . . . "

"Well we'll just have to prove it to you," I said.

"Hopefully," Luna added. "Now if you two are done flirting, can we get going?"

I gave her a quick glare, my gaze hesitating as Martha appeared in the back seat. I quickly turned around, then instructed Max on where to go. There were a few acres of woods between my neighborhood and the next. It seemed the ideal place to start setting traps, and to search for Spooky.

It only took us a few minutes to reach the first location.

Max shut off the engine, and we all hesitated for a moment, knowing the cold would seem even more severe after the warmth of the Jeep. I hadn't expected such a drastic drop in temperature for at least a few weeks.

Luna was the first brave soul to open her door, letting the chill air in. Martha popped out after her.

I looked to Max. "Let's make this quick."

He nodded. "I'll grab the traps. You and your sister figure out where you want to place them."

I flashed him a quick smile then hurried out of the Jeep before I could think twice about it. My legs erupted with goosebumps beneath my jeans, crawling up my skin under the warmth of my coat.

Luna was already waiting on my side of the Jeep, staring out into the darkness. Tall pines loomed in the distance like silent sentinels, their upper needles reflecting the light of the moon.

I glanced at my sister, then started walking, focusing more with my intuition than with my eyes or ears. The night felt alive, though I didn't sense any powerful magic nearby.

With Luna silently keeping pace at my side, we reached the tree line.

A shiver went up my spine. The living quality of the night had increased from the feeling of fluttering moth wings to a swarm of locusts. "There's something here. Can you feel it?"

She nodded. "Magic, but it doesn't feel dark. Just powerful."

Martha floated up beside us, her arms wrapped

tightly around her transparent form. "It feels strange out here."

The three of us turned at the sound of footsteps behind us. Max carried three traps, a larger one in each hand, and a smaller one under his arm. They were the type with pressure plates inside one end, and trap doors on the other. Once an animal walked far enough inside, they would trigger the pressure plate and be trapped, alive and unharmed. None of the traps seemed small enough to catch a mouse, maybe a large rat would be heavy enough to trigger the smallest of the three traps.

Max's face looked a bit ghostly in the moonlight framed by his stocking cap. "Where do you want them?"

I noticed a bag of marshmallows in one of the larger traps. "Are we planning a cookout after this?"

He grinned. "You'd be surprised how many animals will go into a trap after marshmallows. Especially raccoons or opossums."

With a soft laugh, I turned back to the trees. Other than the occasional small animal darting through the underbrush, there was no movement, but the sensation of magic lingered.

"Let's walk a little farther in," I decided.

Luna gave me a wary glance, probably wanting to ask if I was crazy to go in search of whatever magical being awaited us, but it seemed too good of an opportunity to pass up. If whatever was here was the thing making these animals glow with magic, we needed to find out. I wished

I could tell Martha to scout on ahead, but there was no way to speak to her with Max around.

When it became clear that Luna wasn't about to go first either, I led the way, stepping cautiously in case I happened upon a snake. The night seemed to grow darker the further we went, although it was just the effect of the branches overhead blocking out the moon-light. I considered using the flashlight feature on my phone, but that might scare away any animals we hoped to trap.

When we were far enough that I could no longer see the distant neighborhood behind us through the trees, I stopped. "Here should be good."

Max set to work, walking around the area and setting the three traps in different places. After pinning back the doors, he would toss a few marshmallows into the other end near the pressure plate. Martha followed him around, silently observing.

When he was done, he returned to us, unknowingly bringing Martha with him. "We'll need to move before any animals come sniffing this way. I'd recommend just leaving the traps until morning."

I pursed my lips. I was freezing my butt off, but I didn't like the idea of going home without making any real progress. Plus I could still sense magic out here, I just couldn't think of a good excuse to give Max for us to walk deeper into the woods.

Before I could say anything, he stepped closer to me,

his gaze cast outward. He lowered his voice, "I think I saw something move out there."

Hearing his words, Luna scurried toward us and clutched my arm as we all peered into the darkness.

I caught a hint of movement, the sway of a black coat as someone took off running. Without thinking, I pulled away from Luna and took off after them.

"Addy!" I heard Max call, followed by his footsteps pounding behind mine.

I couldn't look back. I caught a glimpse of a figure dressed in black, weaving through the trees ahead. I could sense this person's magic. Maybe they were another witch, or maybe something else. Either way, they had been watching us, and I intended to find out why.

A glowing light caught my attention to my left and I almost ran right into a tree. The animal was the size and shape of a cat, and it was chasing after the same person I was.

"Spooky!" I gasped, changing direction to go after the cat instead of the person.

He didn't seem to hear me. He shot off after our quarry like a miniature comet.

At least now I had something easy to follow, because Spooky was glowing as bright as the moon.

CHAPTER ELEVEN

My lungs started to burn as Spooky's light grew distant. Whoever we were chasing must've been a marathon runner, because they had outpaced me by a mile. I slowed under the weight of my protesting body and utter defeat.

Max caught up, panting heavily and peering through the trees. "We lost your sister back there, she said she couldn't run anymore." He removed his stocking cap and wiped sweat from his brow. "Am I mistaken, or was a glowing animal chasing that person?"

My burning throat felt tight. "It was Spooky."

Max's eyes widened. "There is something exceedingly strange going on here. Why was that person watching us? And why was your cat glowing?"

I shook my head, still staring off into the darkness. "I wish I knew." While I didn't have the answer to any of his questions, I had a sneaking suspicion the person we'd chased had something to do with the glowing animals, and they might have something to do with the dark magic. Why else would they have been watching us? And why would they run?

I started to turn away to search for Luna and Martha, but caught sight of a distant light. I watched for a moment, realizing it was coming toward us.

"Spooky!" I rasped.

Though my legs felt like Jell-O, I rushed toward my familiar, meeting him halfway. I knelt down and he leapt into my arms, giving me an up close look at his glowing fur. Well, not just his fur. The glow emanated from his entire body, like a white aura.

Max caught back up to me, his eyes all for Spooky. "*That* is not normal."

I hugged the cat against my chest. "Tell me about it. Let's get him back to the Jeep."

We both turned to find Luna plodding after us with Martha floating beside her. Luna gasped as I turned with Spooky in my arms, then rushed forward. "Where did you find him!"

"He was chasing the person who was spying on us," I explained. "I never got a good look at them."

She looked from Max to me, probably wondering what explanation I had given him. "When I lost sight of you, I went back to the traps. We caught a glowing rat, though I'm not sure we need it now." She gestured toward Spooky.

"We'll pick it up on our way back," I decided, then started walking.

Max hurried after me. "What do you intend to do? We should report this to someone. What if they're, I don't know, radioactive?"

I turned, holding Spooky close. I had been forced to tell Logan my secret, but I wanted to avoid admitting everything to Max if I could. Something told me he wouldn't quite believe me. "I think we should keep this a secret if we can. We don't need any media involved. Twilight Hollow would be swarmed with people looking for glowing animals. They would trash the woods and annoy the locals."

"But what if these animals are dangerous?" he pressed.

"This is my home, Max. If I can protect it from becoming a madhouse, I will. Just give me a chance to figure this out."

He huffed, fogging the air with his breath. "At least let me look over both animals to make sure they don't pose a danger to you."

I knew the cat gently panting in my arms was no threat, but he could look at the rat if he wanted to. "Deal. Now let's get out of the cold before someone loses a toe."

I stumbled a few times on the way back to the traps. I must have really pushed my body to its limits with the way I'd run. How had that other person moved so quickly?

We reached the traps, and sure enough there was a

glowing rat inside the smallest one. The thing huddled in the back corner of the cage. These animals definitely weren't dangerous. I didn't think they were even aware of what had happened to them.

Max cautiously approached the cage, then knelt down. "This is so weird," he muttered, then looked over his shoulder at me. "Are you sure about this?"

I answered with a sharp nod.

With a heavy sigh, he picked up the trap, staring at the glowing critter within.

Luna sidled up to him. "Why don't you let me take that one? I don't see any reason to leave the two large traps out here."

He carefully handed her the trap, then went to gather the other two.

Martha floated back and forth impatiently, muttering about the odd feeling in the woods.

I still felt it too, that hint of magic, but more distant now. The person we'd chased had taken their magic with them.

With everybody ready to go, I hoisted Spooky more securely in my arms and started walking, wondering if I should tell Logan about any of this. Maybe he was better off not knowing.

Max walked at my side, spooked by my cat, but not by me. If he had any idea what he was dealing with, would he run the other way?

I'd rather not find out.

CHAPTER TWELVE

"Well, they both seem perfectly healthy," Max concluded, stepping away from the dining room chair where we had set the rat in its trap. "The rat's behavior doesn't suggest that it has any diseases, but we can't be sure, so make sure it doesn't bite you."

He rubbed his tired eyes, then glanced at Spooky waiting patiently on the table. The cat had eaten dinner, and Luna had stepped outside to call our mom and Callie.

I watched Max with my arms crossed. "Thanks for this, seriously. Thanks for trusting me about keeping things quiet."

He offered me the ghost of a smile. "I still think we should report this . . . though to whom, I'm not sure. But you're the one who brought me in, not the other way around. It's your choice."

Spooky trotted across the table and nudged Max's hand.

Max hesitated for a moment, then stroked a hand down the cat's back. While his palm was on Spooky's fur it was enveloped in the glow, but as soon as he removed it, his hand appeared normal.

He stared at the cat, then shook his head. "Nope, can't get used to it."

I laughed. "At least you're not the one who has to figure out how to hide a glowing cat. Hopefully it's something that will fade over time."

"Yeah, I don't envy you that." He yawned. "Are you sure you and Luna are okay here with the animals?"

I nodded. "Are you sure you're okay to drive home? You seem like you're about to fall asleep on your feet."

"I'll be fine." He hesitated like he wanted to say more, then thought better of it. "Call me if you need anything, or if either animal starts acting strangely."

With one last look at the animals, he turned and led the way toward the front door. I saw him out, saying a final goodbye before shutting the door behind him and leaning my back against it.

I let out a long sigh as Martha appeared before me.

Her eyes sparkled with excitement, if a ghost's eyes could sparkle. "*Finally*. Your sister is still on the phone and I'm dying to know who that person was in the woods."

I leaned more heavily against the door. "Well I can't really help you there, I have no idea. But they were someone with strong magic. That's what you were sensing in the woods. My sister and I could feel it too."

Her eyes widened. "Another witch?"

I shrugged. "Maybe."

I heard the back door open and shut, then Luna came through the kitchen into the living room. "Mom and Callie will come over in the morning to figure out the animals while you and I go to work."

Martha looked back-and-forth between us. "But what about me? What about my murder?"

I rubbed my burning eyes. "Logan is going to try to procure the contract you saw. The rest of us have our own jobs to do."

I walked into the kitchen where Spooky was still sitting on the table, watching the glowing rat. I took a small saucer for water from the cabinet, then found a slightly wilted carrot in my bottom fridge drawer.

"These will have to do, little guy," I said as I approached the cage with the filled water saucer balanced in one palm.

I set both items on the table, then knelt to figure out the trap. I was pretty sure I could just push the door inward while I gave the rat food and water, then it would spring back into place. The rat huddled at the other end of the cage, watching me with beady little eyes.

"Okay, fella," I soothed. "You just stay over there."

I pressed the door in, then slid the water filled saucer toward the rat. When that had gone over smoothly, I reached back for the carrot.

Spooky hissed. I tried to jerk back my hand, but the rat was already scurrying up my arm.

I shrieked and stumbled backward, holding my arm rigidly out from my body. I wanted the creature off of me but didn't want to fling it hard enough to kill it. I spun around as Luna rushed into the room.

She slid to a halt in front of me. "What are you doing!"

The rat clung to my sweater near my elbow, probably just as terrified as I was, while Spooky leaned near the edge of the table, flailing one paw toward the rodent.

I shuffled closer to Luna, extending my arm for her to grab the rat. She started to reach for it, then paused. We both gasped. The glow faded from the rat, seeming to soak through my sweater into my skin. I got a little rush of a memory of a picnic on a beach—a memory that was not my own—then the sensation dissipated.

Luna grabbed the now ordinary rat by the scruff of its neck, then carried it back to the trap, placing it safely inside and letting the door shut.

She turned wide eyes back to me. "What in the name of the goddess was that?"

A fine trembling overtook my body. I wiped my hands on my jeans, trying to rid myself of the strange sensation. "It was the remnant of a spirit. These animals are glowing because remnants of spirits are clinging to them. I saw someone else's memory before it faded away."

Sensing Martha behind me, I turned.

She watched me with her head tilted. "I could see that spirit, but it's gone now."

"Addy bridged the gap to the spirit world," Luna said to my back. "She helped the remaining fragment move on."

"But where did the spirit come from in the first place?" Martha asked. "It wasn't a ghost like me."

I shivered. "There are all sorts of spirits. I assumed whatever was making these animals glow was some sort of nature spirit, but it wasn't, it was human. And human spirits only come from two places. Some are ghosts like you, and some are brought back to this realm as mere fragments of their former selves."

Martha seemed to think about it. "But who brings them back?"

I turned to Luna, knowing she would've already reached the same conclusion.

Our gazes locked.

"A necromancer," I said. "A necromancer would be needed to bring them back."

Luna audibly gulped. "And the necromancer would have good reason to be interested in a channeling witch."

I felt so lightheaded, I had to sit down. I barely managed to pull a chair out from the table, then I plopped down into it.

Spooky, still glowing, blinked his yellow eyes at me from his perch on the tabletop. The spirit had clung to him because he was magical, and the one clinging to the rat had used it to get to me. It wasn't the dark magic sending these animals out where they could be seen. The spirits were doing it, because they were searching for me.

Now understanding what to do, I reached my hand out and stroked it across Spooky's fur. I channeled the spirit into myself, getting a brief flash of memory. A cozy evening, drinking tea with faces I had never known. Then it was gone, and Spooky no longer glowed.

Luna pulled out the chair next to mine and sat. "This is bad, Addy. A necromancer will want to use you. He probably summoned all the spirits just to test your powers, to see if you could really channel."

My gut clenched. "And once he sees that my familiar is no longer glowing, he'll know that I can."

"You two are starting to scare me," Martha said to my back.

"Good," I groaned, pressing my face into my hands. "We should all be scared."

My mind raced trying to put the puzzle pieces together. Had the necromancer summoned the dark magic? Or was it the other way around? Maybe after its first failed attempt to possess me, the dark magic had summoned a necromancer to do the job. But what did any of this have to do with Martha's murder? Was it just a big coincidence that I saw the first glowing animal the day after I met her ghost?

Too many questions, and no answers to speak of. And I needed to start baking for the cafe in a few hours.

Was it even worth the effort? For all I knew, I was a dead witch walking.

CHAPTER THIRTEEN

The next morning came far too soon. Luna left to get ready for work while I was still baking. I drained the last bit of coffee from my cup, then refilled it, hoping my tired brain hadn't forgotten any components of my recipes.

My phone buzzed as I was sliding the final tray of scones into the oven.

I spotted Logan's name on the caller ID, then answered. "Yeah?"

"Someone got up on the wrong side of the broomstick this morning, didn't she? I take it you didn't have much luck with the animals?"

I leaned against the counter. "Oh no, we had plenty of luck, and Spooky is back. I only got a few hours of sleep."

"Did I wake you?"

I knelt in front of the oven to watch the scones.

"Nope, I had to get up early to bake for the cafe. What's up?"

"Based on Martha's suspicions, I did a little bit more research on Alex. He's on the brink of bankruptcy."

My eyebrows shot up. I looked to Spooky sitting on the table, watching me like he was actually listening to my words. "So you think he killed Martha so he could sell the gallery and save himself?"

"I'm not sure the gallery is worth enough to save him, but it's a start. And Martha had left him her remaining holdings, minus the house going to Blake."

I gnawed my lip, thinking it over. "Martha hadn't mentioned that. I'll ask her about it. She should be floating around here somewhere."

"Let me know what she says. Now what happened with the animals?"

I rolled my eyes, though he couldn't see it. "You only just shared this information with me because you wanted me to feel obligated into being honest with you, didn't you?"

"Did it work, do you feel obligated?"

I wished he could see my glare. "Come by the cafe later, I'll tell you in person." *After I talk with my sisters and figure out how much I should tell you,* I added silently.

"I have a few things to wrap up, then I'll see you there."

We said our goodbyes and hung up, then I looked

back to Spooky. "I hope you know you're coming to work with me today on a leash."

He narrowed his yellow eyes.

"No arguing," I lectured, then looked down to the rat still in the cage. "We can drop you off on the way."

He blinked his little black eyes. I was pretty sure he was just a normal rat again.

Martha popped up right beside me. "And then we can go see Blake."

I raised a hand to my pounding heart. "Geez, don't just pop up like that. Why do you want to go see Blake? And where have you been?"

She floated over to examine my packaged up muffins on the opposite counter. "I was following the detective, I heard his end of the conversation. I had completely forgotten the specifics of my will, I had it drawn up so long ago. I never told Alex that I left everything to him. But Blake did know he was getting the house. It had belonged to both me and his mother, so I promised I would leave it to him."

I watched her back, unable to see her face even though she was transparent. Ghosts were weird like that, you could see through them, but you couldn't just see through the back to the front. "I thought you were so sure it was Alex who killed you."

Her shoulders slumped as she hung her head. "I was worked up after I found the contract, but I've had a lot of time to think about it. I just can't imagine him doing this to me."

"But you could imagine your nephew doing it?"

She disappeared, then reappeared facing me. She really was getting the hang of this ghost thing. "Blake and I were never terribly close, and he lost his mother a long time ago. I can't be sure he wouldn't do this if he was desperate enough. The house is worth a lot."

My timer beeped for the scones, and I turned and took them out of the oven. "All right, Blake's pawnshop is on the way. It might not be open this early, but he does often come in for a cup of coffee." *And to flirt mercilessly.* I had only ever talked him up to get information about Neil Howard's murder, but apparently it had been enough encouragement for him to start visiting the cafe.

This seemed to appease Martha, and I left the scones to cool while I went upstairs and got dressed.

Given the sudden chill, I opted for a white fisherman's sweater that was just formfitting enough to be worn beneath my down coat. I added dark-wash jeans, waterproof boots, pulled my curls into a braid, and I was good to go.

By the time I had packed up the baked goods, the cat, and the rat into my car it was 6:45. I'd have to be quick dropping off the rat if I was going to make it to open the cafe in time.

With Spooky sitting in the passenger seat, the rejected collar and leash I had purchased when I first found him sitting forlornly on the floorboard, I started the engine and blasted the heat.

The cat peered contentedly at the rat in its trap in

the back seat, as if we hadn't just had a horrible non-verbal argument over him wearing the collar and leash.

We made the short drive to the edge of the neighborhood, then I quickly got out and grabbed the rat. I shut the door, trapping Spooky inside the car. This was one argument I wasn't losing. I wasn't about to have him run off after another glowing animal.

Because there *were* more animals with spirits clinging to them out in the trees. I could feel them as I walked with the trap under one arm. I found myself wishing Martha had remained with me rather than going to watch Logan again. She might be able to sense something out here I couldn't.

By the time I reached the trees, I was glad I had worn the waterproof boots. The slowly melting frost on the grass left beads of moisture behind.

I held the trap out in front of me and looked down at the rat. "I hope you'll be all right in the cold. Try not to run into any necromancers."

I shivered at the thought, then knelt down and released the rat from his trap. He scurried off into the underbrush, and I stood, holding the trap in one hand while rubbing the goosebumps beneath my coat with the other.

Under the light of day, the feeling of spirits in the woods was fainter, but it was definitely still there, and it called to me. Maybe that was the necromancer's plan. Use the lure of spirits needing to be sent back to draw the channeling witch out alone into the woods.

With another shiver, I turned and hurried back toward the car, running by the time I drew close to it. I wouldn't be going out alone into the woods any time soon. It felt like there were eyes on me my entire retreat.

I hopped into the car and threw the trap in the back.

Stupid, a voice chided in my mind.

I turned wide eyes to Spooky, who was staring at me from the passenger seat. "Did you say something?"

When all I got was a continued stare in reply, I shook my head and started the car. It was only a few minutes to seven. Even if Blake was open early, I would have to talk to him later.

The drive to the cafe only took a few minutes, and maybe I had willed Blake to visit, because he was waiting right outside the front door along with Elmer and Francis.

I parked on the street and opened my car door, then cursed when Spooky leapt out before I could stop him, making it clear the collar and leash were a lost cause. I got out and greeted my three customers, then unlocked the door for them.

Blake held it open for Elmer and Francis, then I stopped him with a hand on his arm before he could follow them in. "Do you think you could help me carry a few trays of muffins?" I mustered a charming smile, though I wasn't really a fan of his advances.

He pushed his shaggy blonde hair away from his face and grinned. "Of course, little lady."

It was good Blake couldn't read minds, or he

would've run away at my thoughts over being called a *little lady*. Unfortunately, I couldn't read minds either, so it would take a little bit of charm and an extra large magic coffee to find out anything he might know about his aunt's death.

All in a day's work for a channeling, mystery solving witch.

CHAPTER FOURTEEN

Blake slid the last tray of muffins onto the countertop. "You baked all this today?" he asked, watching me on the other side of the counter as I arranged cookies in the glass display case.

I nodded, focused on my task.

"What, did you wake up at two in the morning?"

"Five," I muttered, giving the white chocolate macadamia nut cookies center placement. "As long as I time things right and I'm always mixing up the next batch while the last one is baking, I can get it all done." I cast a quick glance around for Spooky, noticing him licking his paw on top of one of the bookshelves.

Finished with the cookies, I reached for the last tray of muffins. They would stay hidden behind the counter until room was freed up in the case.

Blake drummed his fingers on the counter. Despite his profession, he had rough working man's hands with faint unscrubbable dirt under the nails. Maybe from the camping and fishing he did in his free time.

"Did you want a coffee?" I asked to fill the awkward silence. "It's on the house for helping me."

Elmer and Francis both pretended not to watch us from their table near the door. I had made their coffees first thing so they wouldn't have to wait.

"A coffee would be great." Blake winked.

I forced a smile, preparing myself to flirt. It wasn't that Blake was an unattractive man. His hair was a nice shade of blonde, and he was fit from hiking. He was five or six years older than me, not too huge of an age gap once you were in your thirties. He owned his own business . . . but he was just too . . . Blake. He was like the cheesy uncle that cornered you and told bad jokes at holiday gatherings.

I kept a muted version of my smile in place while I fixed his coffee in a to-go cup, then slid it across the counter. "I was sorry to hear about your aunt, by the way."

I hoped it wouldn't be taken as odd that I knew the information. Her death had been on the local news, and a few people around town seemed to know she was his aunt. Word traveled fast.

Fortunately, he didn't seem to question it. "We weren't close. Once my mom, her sister, passed away, we didn't really keep in touch other than the occasional holiday visit." He took his coffee and stepped back.

Oh no you don't, I thought. *You're not getting out of*

here that fast. "I heard you were one of her only remaining blood relatives."

He laughed, moving a little closer to the counter again. "People sure do talk in this town, don't they? But yeah, I don't come from a big family. It's worked out in my favor though. My aunt left me her portion of the house she shared with my mom. It's worth a decent amount of cash." He leaned one hand on the counter while holding his coffee with the other.

It was clear he expected me to be impressed he had inherited some wealth.

"Well that is fortunate," I said with a smile. "What happened to the rest of her holdings? Did she leave them to a friend?"

He snorted. "Her best friend Cheryl would've loved to have some cash, I'm sure, but it all went to my aunt's ex-husband."

I furrowed my brow. Why would Cheryl need cash? "Has her friend fallen on hard times?"

He shrugged his bony shoulders. "She's been trying to pawn stuff at my shop for the past couple months, so I assume so. I had to send her to Wickenburg for most of it, not a big market for old paintings in Twilight Hollow. I wouldn't even know how to value them."

"Old paintings?" I blurted.

He narrowed an eye, and I worried I'd gone too far. "You like art then?"

I heaved a subtle sigh of relief. "Yes, I like art. What kind of paintings were they?"

He shrugged again. "Landscapes, portraits, you name it. Even some of that stuff that looks like a toddler painted it. If you like art, you should go check out my departed aunt's gallery. It's over in Wickenburg."

"I just might do that," I smiled.

"We could always go together."

My smile faltered, and I quickly turned and started making myself a coffee to hide it. "I'll have to get back to you on that. As you can see, I'm pretty busy with baking and running the cafe." I gestured with one hand to the display case.

"Well you just let me know. Maybe it's time to hire some help."

I glanced back at him. "You know, people keep telling me that."

The bell on the door rang as a trio of older ladies stepped inside, their cheeks flushed from the cold.

Blake seemed to take this as his cue to leave. He gestured with his coffee cup in my direction. "Thanks for the coffee, I'll see you around."

I waved as he walked off, then moved toward the register to meet my new customers. The smile I gave them was genuine, not only because I was grateful to all my customers, but because I had learned something important from Blake. Many somethings. First off, Cheryl was broke. Second, she had been trying to sell paintings, which was a bit odd given her best friend owned a gallery. Wouldn't she have just sold the paintings to Martha?

And third, Blake was pretty excited about the cash he was going to get from selling Martha's house. It was a motive, and it was well known that he was an outdoorsman. He might have been able to follow Martha on her hike without her noticing.

Just as I finished taking the ladies' orders and they went to sit down, Logan walked into the cafe.

I gave him a smug smile as he walked toward the register.

He narrowed his eyes at me. "What's that look for?"

I grinned as I started the shots of espresso for the ladies' lattes. "Oh, I just discovered plenty of clues that you probably missed."

"Well that explains me seeing Blake Monroe walking down the street with a cup of coffee and a huge grin." He leaned forward over the counter and lowered his voice. "You know it's not fair when you use your womanly wiles on my suspects."

I braced my elbows on the counter, mirroring his position. "Well then you ought to get better at questioning them."

I sensed eyes boring into my skull, and glanced to see Francis watching me over her coffee cup, a devilish grin taking up half her face.

I rolled my eyes at her. Sometimes I wondered if I stayed single just to spite Francis. She probably wondered the same.

Logan followed my gaze, helping him realize we had an audience. "Can we go into your office?"

I turned to start steaming the milk. "I didn't expect you to get here so quickly, you're going to have to wait until after the morning rush."

As if to emphasize my point, a college-aged couple walked through the front door.

"I'll wait," Logan said, stepping away from the counter to make room. "Can I get a coffee when you have a chance?"

I gave him a little salute, then turned to greet my next customers. Everything was a blur from there on out. By the time I made the last beverage, the display case was half empty and all the tables were filled.

At one of the smaller tables sat Logan, a cup of coffee I'd managed to bring him in one hand. With him sat Max, who I hadn't realized was even there because he hadn't come up to order yet. Spooky had come down from his bookshelf to sit in Max's lap, so the cat was officially out of the bag, as it were. Max knew the cat was no longer glowing, and he might want to know why.

I chewed my lip, wondering what the two men were talking about as another customer approached the counter.

"Earth to Addy," Richie said, snapping his fingers in front of my face.

I tore my gaze away from Max and Logan, giving Richie my full attention. "Sorry, it was quite the morning rush, I'm a little dazed."

I glanced back toward Logan's table. They were both smiling, that had to be good, right? Surely they weren't talking about glowing animals, and whatever I wasn't telling them about said glowing animals.

"You know, I'm around if you need to hire someone else."

I turned my attention back to Richie to find him grinning at me.

I frowned. "Don't you have class?"

He shrugged his leather jacket up on his shoulders. "Only a few hours a day, and I'm free first thing in the morning. I could help you with the rush."

I thought about it. Evie had to stick to a particular schedule because of her daughter. It might be nice to have someone to cover for me whenever things were crazy in my life, which seemed to be all the time lately.

"How about a trial run right now?" I asked, glancing again toward Logan and Max.

Richie was around the counter next to the register before I could think twice about it. "You won't regret this, Addy."

Grinning and shaking my head, I made Max a coffee before leaving Richie behind the counter. Perhaps at another cafe the owner might be worried the customers would be intimidated by Richie's overall tough look, but not at the Toasty Bean. My customers could get their coffee from an alleged witch, a street kid who was actually a gentle college student, or Evie . . . who wasn't really a misfit however you looked at it.

As I approached Max and Logan with Max's coffee, I realized I had already convinced myself that I would hire Richie. There were few people I would trust more.

Both men looked up at me as I reached them, and I realized they had been talking about me, judging by their sudden silence.

Logan was the first to speak. "Max tells me your cat was glowing last night." He gestured toward the cat in Max's lap.

I aimed a quick glare Max's way.

He held up his hands. "He said he knew you were going to try to trap the animals. I figured he knew about . . . the rest of it."

I pursed my lips, but handed him his coffee. It was a reasonable explanation, but now I was going to have to explain to Logan why Spooky was no longer glowing. I knew Max probably wouldn't push me too hard for answers, but Logan would, and I still wasn't sure what I wanted to tell him.

My problems doubled when the next person walked into the cafe.

My mom was tall and thin, but seemed to take up more space than her wiry frame required. She removed her lavender parka, raked fingers through her ginger curls, then aimed brown eyes at me. "Adelaide O'Shea, we need to talk."

I groaned as she moved closer to me. "Luna called you, didn't she?"

"Of course she did." She looked down at both the men watching us. "You," she pointed to Logan. "I want to speak with you first." She looked to Max. "You make sure Adelaide doesn't run away while I'm not looking."

She turned and walked toward my office, leaving no room for arguments.

I gave Logan a grimace. "You better follow her. You don't want to make her mad."

Logan quickly obeyed, leaving me alone with Max.

I slumped into Logan's vacated seat with a heavy sigh. "I suppose you want to know what happened with the animals after you left."

He nodded encouragingly, and I willed my tired brain to come up with something believable to say. I hated lying. I wasn't good at it, and it gave me a nervous feeling in my stomach, but in this situation I saw no other way.

So I lifted my chin, stiffened my jaw, and lied through my teeth.

CHAPTER FIFTEEN

"So the glow just went away?" Max searched my face, probably trying to tell if I was lying. Spooky had vacated his lap to go back to his bookshelf.

I shrugged. "When I woke up this morning, both the animals were fine. I dropped the rat off on my way to work. I have your trap in my car by the way."

He sipped his coffee, then placed his cup on the table. "Maybe we should set the traps again to get a better look at any other glowing animals before it fades."

Think Addy, think. I shrugged. "I think it seems pretty harmless. Maybe it's just some form of bioluminescent organism."

His eyes went distant for a moment in thought. "But why would it die off so suddenly?"

"Maybe because we brought the animals inside?"

He pursed his lips. "Maybe, but if this is a new

undocumented organism, I really would like to know more about it."

I couldn't think of anything else to say. It was clear I wasn't going to steer him off this path. I was saved as my mother and Logan emerged from my office past the bookshelves. Logan had on his unreadable cop expression, and my mom looked unhappy.

I found myself dying to know what they had talked about.

Logan reached the table first, ignoring Max and looking down at me. "Your mom filled me in, now I need to get back to work."

I opened my mouth to argue, but he patted my shoulder and walked toward the door, leaving an opening for my mom to address me.

She put her hands on her hips and gestured with her chin back toward the office. "You next, Adelaide."

Max scooted out his chair. "That's my cue to leave."

Looking at my mom's stern expression, I couldn't blame him for fleeing. "Save yourself," I said to him.

He stood. "I'll call you later." He turned to my mom. "Nice seeing you again."

She gave him a brief smile, showing him that she was mad at me, not him, then Max escaped, leaving me alone with my mother. Well, alone with my mother and a cafe full of people. I glanced toward Richie, seeming completely at home with the cash register as he rung up a customer's order.

My mom tapped her foot on the wood floor. "Let's go, Adelaide."

I sighed, and stood. I was pretty sure that Evie had been teaching Richie the register while I was away from the cafe. It seemed the choice to hire him wasn't entirely my own.

I followed my mom into the office, holding the door open long enough for Spooky to hop down from his shelf and join us.

Once we were alone my mom gestured for me to sit behind my desk while she stayed standing.

She crossed her arms and looked down at me with Spooky twining around her legs. "You shouldn't have taken in the spirit fragments, Adelaide. Any time you channel any part of a spirit or ghost, it has the potential to possess you."

"It's not like I had a choice," I argued. "It just happened. As soon as the rat touched me the glow left it. And I'm fine now, by the way. Thanks for asking."

She sucked her teeth, mulling over my words. "Luna says you both believe a necromancer is behind this. Ida agrees."

My jaw dropped. "You talked to Ida?" After my mom's long-dead sister had briefly possessed me, we hadn't seen her again. My mom thought the ordeal had weakened her too much to make contact with the living.

She nodded. "She's back, and she senses a new power in town. She's not sure if this new person is working with the dark magic, or if they were simply lured by it, but either way she's scared. No ghost or witch is safe with a necromancer around."

I leaned my elbows on the desk, bracing my chin in my hand. "So what do we do?"

"We stick together, and we find this necromancer."

I narrowed my eyes. "What exactly do you mean by stick together?"

I already knew what was coming before she said it.

"You need to come stay with me, Adelaide. You're not safe by yourself, and your sisters can't watch you all the time. This is more than just the dark magic. If that dark force is working with a necromancer, they're both coming for you."

Even though I'd been expecting her words, my stomach plummeted to my feet. I loved my mom, I really did, but we'd never fully seen eye to eye. I'd fought hard for my independence, and anything that threatened it made me feel like a glowing rat in a trap.

"You know I'm right," she pressed. "A necromancer would want to use your connection to the other side to draw greater spirits into this realm. It's not just your safety on the line."

I buried my head in my hands. She was right. Whatever this necromancer had planned wasn't bad for just me. "Fine," I groaned. "Spooky and I will head over before dark."

"I'm glad you can see reason. Now you have a visitor, I'll leave you to speak with her."

I lifted my head enough to watch my mom leaving the office, wondering what she meant about a visitor.

I found out just a second later as Martha popped up right where my mom had been standing.

"How long have you been spying?" I asked.

Martha crossed her arms and lifted her nose. "I followed the detective here. We saw Blake on the street leaving the cafe. Did you learn anything from him?"

I almost wanted to shout at her that I had bigger problems than her murder, but managed to contain myself. "Well, Blake was pretty excited to inherit your house, or actually to inherit the cash he'll get from selling it. He also implied that Cheryl is broke. She's been pawning her belongings, including several paintings."

She floated closer to the desk, looking down at me. "But Cheryl doesn't have any paintings of value, and if she did, why wouldn't she come to me? I could have gotten her the best price for them."

I shook my head. "I don't know, but it's suspicious."

"That settles it then. We need to pay her another visit."

I stood. "What I need to do is get back to work. I'll call Logan and tell him what I learned, and he can go question Cheryl about it."

Martha nodded sharply. "I would appreciate if you could call him now."

I saw no reason not to, so I leaned to one side and drew my phone out of my pocket, scrolling through the contacts and picking Logan's name. After six rings I got his voicemail and left a message for him to call me back.

Martha's eyes darted around the office impatiently, settling on the cat now sitting on my desk. "What am I supposed to do until he calls you back?"

I stood and moved toward the door. "I don't know, go spy on Cheryl. Check back with me in a couple hours and hopefully I will have heard from him."

With a huff, she disappeared, and I was free to go back out into the cafe to do my job. I might as well spend the rest of the morning training Richie on anything Evie hadn't gotten to. If I was going to be hiding out at my mom's, I would need him now more than ever.

Hopefully we could find the necromancer and deal with him quickly, and life could go back to normal.

Or as normal as the life of a witch could get.

CHAPTER SIXTEEN

As the hours ticked on, I left two more messages for Logan. Things were slow at 4 PM, so I decided to close up early so I could pack for my mom's before dark.

Martha popped up just as I was locking the front door with Spooky standing at my heels.

"Cheryl was at work all day," she explained. "What a bore. Have you heard from the detective?"

I turned with my keys in hand and glanced both ways down the street, making sure no one was close enough to see me talking to myself. "I left two more messages, but he hasn't called me back. I wonder if my mom said something to him to keep him away."

Martha crossed her arms, hovering just above the sidewalk. "Well then you'll just have to go question Cheryl. I cannot wait another night. I feel—"

Her gaze went distant, and I realized why she was suddenly being more insistent.

"You're beginning to fade, aren't you?" I asked. "You're losing your grip on this realm."

She shrugged her spectral shoulders. "I'm not sure, I just know that I feel strange. Like I'm losing pieces of myself."

A gust of wind sent dead leaves skittering across the sidewalk around my boots. It got dark early this time of year. I either had time to pack, or to visit Cheryl, not both.

"Can you tell how much longer you have?" I asked.

Her brow creased as she thought about it. "I'm not sure, but I'm inclined to think not long. I don't want to go without knowing who killed me, Addy."

Her pleading tone pushed me the last inch toward my decision. "All right, we'll go speak to Cheryl. But we have to make it quick, I need to get out to my mom's before dark."

She gave me a sad smile. "You're a true friend, Addy."

Hopefully I don't end up a dead friend, I thought. "Let's go then, we're burning daylight."

She followed me to my car, melting her way into the back seat. I sat Spooky beside me in the front and started the engine, then tried giving Logan one last call.

Still no answer. If he was avoiding me on purpose, I was going to get angry. Angry enough to not tell him I was on my way to question Cheryl. I hung up before the voicemail greeting could finish, then started driving.

Along the way I finally gave in and left messages for Callie and Luna, telling them I was stopping by Cheryl's before heading out to mom's, and also inviting them to come to mom's too. If I had to stay out in the woods with my mom, I at least wanted my sisters along as a buffer.

Martha remained silent for the drive, and I wondered just how much of herself she had already lost. It was normal for ghosts to fade unless they had some sort of strong connection to the living world. Sometimes they could attach themselves to objects, or like Ida, to a place. Some held on wanting vengeance, or justice. The need for justice was what had made Martha hold on for this long, but it wasn't strong enough to keep her here forever. Eventually she would fade, and we would no longer have her input on the investigation.

Not only that, but she would never learn who killed her. Maybe it didn't matter wherever she was going, but it felt wrong not to give her answers so she could be at peace.

My thoughts carried me all the way to Cheryl's where my car crunched up the gravel drive.

I parked and shut off the engine, glancing back at Martha. "Any advice on how to broach the subject?"

She shrugged. "As is the case in many situations, the truth might be the best option. Tell her you're friends with my nephew, and he mentioned that she had been trying to sell paintings."

I took a studying breath, preparing for the confrontation ahead, then opened my door and got out of the car. I let Spooky follow me out. If anything bad happened, I wanted him near me.

Martha disappeared as I approached the front door. She had probably gone ahead into the house to see Cheryl's reaction at my reappearance.

Cheryl opened the door before I could knock, looking me up and down. There were dark marks beneath her eyes. She still wore her slacks and silk blouse from work, stocking-clad feet visible atop the wooden floor of the entryway.

"Detective," she said pleasantly, "can I help you?"

I stared at her dumbly for a second, then realized that we had never clarified who I was when we first came to question her. She just knew I came with the other detective, and probably assumed I was his partner. It was illegal to impersonate an officer, but was it really that bad if I just didn't correct her?

"I just have a few more questions for you. Do you mind if I come in?"

She stepped back and opened the door further, revealing Martha hovering a few paces behind her.

I stepped inside. It was getting dark enough that she didn't seem to notice Spooky slipping in through the door behind me.

Cheryl shut the door, then walked into the sitting room, giving me her back for a moment, long enough for Spooky to trot in the other direction further into her house.

"I was just fixing my dinner," Cheryl explained as she turned back to me. "But I have a few minutes."

I stepped into the sitting room, feeling a bit wary about what I was doing. It was probably a mistake to come and question Cheryl on my own. I didn't really know her, or what she was capable of. If she really was the murderer, she could be dangerous.

I watched her expression turn wary, realizing my thoughts had shown too much on my face. Best to cut right to the chase then, before she could kick me out. "How familiar are you with Blake Monroe and his business, Golden Dollar Pawn?"

Her eyes widened, just a fraction, but enough to be noticeable. "Blake was Martha's nephew, but I'm not overly familiar with him or his shop."

Maybe I should have tried to be clever to get her to admit something, but full dark wasn't far off. There just wasn't enough time. "That's odd, because he just told me that you've been trying to sell stuff to him for months, including many paintings." I left it at that, no accusations, not yet.

Her mouth opened and shut like a fish gasping for air until she took a shaky breath, then shuffled her feet toward a cushioned chair. She sat down and looked up at me. "I know this looks bad, but it's not what you think. I'll admit that I'm broke, but I haven't done anything wrong except try to save my pride."

Martha hovered near her friend's seat. "Ask her about the paintings," she whispered.

I flicked my eyes to Martha, then back to Cheryl. "What sort of things were you trying to sell?"

She chewed her lip, deciding what to say. Probably wondering if Blake had already told me.

I took a seat across from her and waited.

"It's really not what you think," she blurted. "The paintings were mine to sell."

"Where did you get them?"

She looked around the room, as if something within could save her.

"Cheryl," I pressed, "I can't help you unless you tell me the truth."

That did it. She broke down into tears. "Alright, I'll admit it," she sobbed. "I found the paintings in storage at Martha's gallery when I was visiting her one weekend. She had given me the keys to pick something up for her. The gallery was closed, no one was around, and the paintings were just there under some sheets. I figured if they weren't out on the floor, they weren't particularly special and no one would miss them. I needed the cash, so I took them and tried to sell them."

I leaned forward with my elbows on my knees, giving her a sympathetic expression, willing her to go on.

She wiped tears from her eyes. "When Blake didn't want to buy them, I took them to a pawnshop in the city. The owner looked one of the paintings up, and it turns out it was stolen. Not just by me, but by Martha or whoever put them in the gallery. I turned tail and ran, leaving the paintings behind."

"You little rat," Martha muttered, shaking her head.

I gestured to the painting on the wall. "What about that one?"

Her eyebrows shot up. "Oh no, that one I actually purchased from the gallery. I felt so bad about what I had done, I wanted to somehow contribute to Martha's business. I saw the piece posted online, and had Martha's employee send it right over. He said it was a new aquisition. I paid double the value. I was going to surprise Martha when she got back from her hike."

She hung her head as fresh tears welled up. "But she never came back."

Martha lifted her gaze from her friend to shake her head at me. "We would never have stolen paintings in the gallery. Everything is vetted beforehand."

"Cheryl?" I said softly.

She lifted her head, blinking back more tears.

"Where do you think the stolen paintings came from? Why were they in the gallery to begin with?"

She frowned, as if she hadn't thought that far ahead. "Only three people have access to that back room in the gallery. Martha, Alex, and Jackson, their employee. Martha was many things, but most certainly not a criminal. It had to be either Alex or Jackson."

I thought about it. I didn't really know much about Jackson, except that he hoped to eventually open his own gallery. And Alex, he'd fallen on hard times. He definitely had a motive for moving stolen art.

The room had grown darker as we talked, and I realized full dark had fallen without me noticing. My mom would be wondering where I was.

I stood. "Thank you for your time, Cheryl."

She blinked at me. "You mean you're not going to arrest me for stealing those paintings from the gallery?"

Ah, not very detective-like of me. "You may have just given me useful information in solving Martha's murder. We can forget about the paintings, for now."

"Oh thank you," she sobbed. "Please just figure out who did this to Martha."

I noticed Spooky slinking toward the front door and shuffled to one side to block Cheryl's view. "I can see myself out. Thanks for your time."

She nodded appreciatively, and I retreated, doing my best to block Spooky from sight as I opened the door and let him run out, then hurried out after him.

The darkness outside felt alive, or maybe it was just my nerves. I looked down at Spooky as Martha popped up next to us, noticing a scrap of paper hanging from his mouth.

I knelt down and he released it into my hand, then read it as I walked toward my car. It was an address I didn't recognize, and I wasn't sure why Spooky had deemed it important, but I could at least look it up. I folded the paper and put it in my back pocket for later.

I reached for my car door when I suddenly sensed a presence at my back.

"Addy!" Martha screamed.

A hand holding a bunched up piece of cloth clamped over my mouth, bringing sharp fumes to fill my airways.

I heard Spooky hissing, someone cursing, and then everything went black.

CHAPTER SEVENTEEN

I woke on my back, staring up the trunks of tall trees. The stars glittered like tiny white sapphires overhead. My feet and hands were numb with cold.

"Wha—" I coughed.

A man's face loomed over me, his skin deathly pale in the moonlight. I placed him somewhere in his early thirties, probably just a year or two younger than me. A mop of dark hair hung forward, shadowing his eyes. I couldn't tell what color they were, something light. "Hello witch."

My voice came out strained and raspy. "Hello necromancer. Where are we?"

One corner of his thin lips ticked up. "That doesn't really matter. I have you here now, right where I want you. My little channeling witch. When I saw your familiar with you tonight, the glow of residual spirits gone, I knew you were the one I've been looking for."

Luna had been right. He had been using the glowing animals to test me, to find out if I could really channel.

"What did you do with Spooky?" I growled. "Where's Martha?"

The necromancer pushed up the sleeve of his black coat, revealing freshly bleeding scratches up and down his arm and wrist. "Your little kitty ran away before I could thrash him. And your ghost fled to save herself."

He backed away as I managed to sit up. I had to pause halfway until my swimming vision stilled. "What do you want from me?"

He crouched beside me, putting us at eye level. "Something powerful lured me here. There is a dark magic in these woods, and I intend to capture it, using you as bait. I imagine it will come looking for you soon."

I closed my eyes and pinched my brow, wincing against the throbbing in my head. "You don't know what you're dealing with. You won't be able to control the dark magic."

I felt his hot breath near my cheek. "We'll see about that. Whatever this magical force is, it wants you, and that makes me believe it is something long dead, and I can control the dead."

I took slow steady breaths, deciding what to do. He was close enough that I might be able to lash out and catch him off guard.

My moment of decision ended as the air shifted with his movement, then his footsteps retreated.

The throbbing in my head eased enough for me to open my eyes.

The necromancer was crouched near a black duffel bag I hadn't noticed in the darkness. He withdrew an athame, a ritual dagger, holding it up so the sharp edge gleamed in the moonlight.

He approached me. "Hold still and I won't have to cut you too deeply."

I skittered away through the dead leaves like a crab, wondering if that line ever worked for him, because I was pretty sure he had done this before. He was way too confident to be a newbie at blood rituals.

If he cut me, he could amplify the magic in my blood and use it to lure all sorts of spirits, including the dark magic. It was a trick not just exclusive to necromancers, any witch or magical being could do it with enough know-how.

He caught up to me and reached down and snatched my wrist. The loose sleeve of my sweater slid down, bunching around my elbow. I tried to push away with my feet, but my legs felt like limp noodles.

He wrenched my arm toward him, poising the blade above my skin.

"Hiss!"

A dark shape dropped down from the tree above him, hissing and scratching. He stumbled back, letting go of my arm.

I watched on in horror as the necromancer flailed his

blade, trying to grab Spooky off the back of his shoulder with his free hand.

Martha popped up beside me. "Run!" she rasped. "You need to run, Addy!"

I used the nearby tree trunk to pull myself to my feet, but I couldn't run, not with Spooky in danger. I wasn't sure if my legs would let me run at all.

I turned myself toward the necromancer as he finally managed to grab Spooky by the scruff of the neck and flung him toward the ground. Anger overcame my fear and I staggered toward him with my fists clenched.

He gripped his athame in one bleeding hand and aimed it my way. "Stay where you are, witch."

I stopped walking as Spooky regained his senses and ran toward me. He was okay. I heaved a sigh of relief, then instantly tensed again. The trees behind the necromancer were filling with glowing green fog, lighting up the forest floor.

The necromancer was so focused on me, he didn't seem to notice it right away. He took a step toward me, blade outstretched.

"You might want to look behind you," I said.

A scratch on his pale cheek started to drip blood. "You won't fool me that easily, witch."

"Then use your senses, necromancer." I nodded behind him.

The green glowing fog was nearly at his heels, and the magical force it brought with it was way more frightening than the necromancer could ever be. I needed to run, but I also needed him to not stab me in the back.

Spooky pressed against my thigh, granting me a bit of strength as the necromancer finally glanced back, then gasped.

He turned toward the dark magic, then gestured back toward me with his knife. "I've brought you the one you want, take her."

Tendrils of the green fog started twining around his ankles like tiny snakes. He stepped back, but the fog filled the void, creeping up toward his knees. The dark magic might want me, but it seemed it wanted the necromancer too.

Run, a voice hissed through my mind.

I glanced down at Spooky, staring up at me, then back to the necromancer now stumbling back from the green fog.

He glanced over his shoulder. "Help me!"

"Let's get out of here," Martha whispered in my ear.

The necromancer tripped and fell to the ground, giving the fog the opportunity to swarm, if something like fog could swarm. It was the best word that came to mind. It fell upon his body, then snaked into his mouth and nostrils.

The magic was going to take him over like it had done to me when Ike chased me into the woods. I wasn't about to hang around until the necromancer got back up.

I turned and ran, stumbling when my legs didn't

want to carry me. I wasn't sure which direction my car was in, or how far away it was. Spooky trotted at my side.

Martha floated past me. "This way!"

Behind me, the necromancer screamed.

Finally the mental fog of whatever he'd used to knock me out lifted, and I managed to run faster, stumbling against trees in the dark as I went.

I fled through the dark woods, chasing after a ghost, with a necromancer and dark magic in the trees behind me.

At least no one could say my life wasn't interesting.

CHAPTER EIGHTEEN

My body was coated in sweat by the time I reached my car. The lights in Cheryl's house were out. She must have never looked outside to make sure I was gone.

My hands trembled as I fumbled my car keys out of my pocket. I held the door open for Spooky to hop in ahead of me, then slid in after him, slamming my hand down on the automatic lock switch as soon as we were shut inside.

I glanced again at Cheryl's cabin. My car engine might wake her and she might realize I'd been parked here all this time, but I'd rather deal with that than a necromancer possessed by dark magic.

I started the engine and hit the gas too hard, kicking up gravel with my tires, then sped down her driveway.

I nearly swerved into a tree as Martha popped up in my back seat. "Where are we going to go? You need to hide. Whoever that man was, I have little doubt he'll come for you. And what was that green fog?"

I tightly gripped the steering wheel with both hands as I drove past dark trees on either side, waiting for the green glow to appear. "Too many questions right now Martha. I need to focus on escaping."

"Well you can't go home. What if he follows you?"

I shivered. She was right. Who knew how long the necromancer had been watching me? He might already know where my mom lived, and he most certainly knew where I lived. And so did the dark magic. No matter which one ended up in control, they could find me, and they would be more powerful now together.

"I have an idea," she said when I didn't answer. "I'm sure my house hasn't been sold off yet. I have a spare key hidden outside. You can go there. No one would know where to find you."

I breathed a sigh of relief as I pulled out onto the highway. No one was following me. "Give me directions."

She did, and I was glad for the distraction of driving to Wickenburg.

The miles passed by, and I began to feel a little safer. I followed Martha's directions, exiting toward Wickenburg and heading into an upper class neighborhood.

I had escaped, for now. I could hide out at Martha's house for a little while and call my mom and sisters to tell them what happened. From there, we could figure out what to do. Thinking of them, I grabbed my phone from the center console, glancing at it to see six missed calls. Alright, maybe I shouldn't wait to call them.

I selected the most recent call from the log, Callie, and dialed her back.

"Thank goddess," she said after answering on the first ring. "We've been worried sick, and neither of us know where Cheryl lives. Logan hasn't answered any of Luna's calls."

I gripped the phone tightly so my trembling hand wouldn't drop it, keeping my eyes on the road. "The necromancer found me. He knocked me out with some chemical, or maybe a spell, and dragged me into the woods. He wanted to use my blood to lure in the dark magic, but it came on its own and attacked him. I didn't hang around to see what happened."

"What!" I had to pull the phone a bit away from my ear at her shriek. "That's it, we're calling mom. We hadn't told her you were missing yet just in case you were fine, but she's going to start wondering why you haven't made it to her house soon."

"Callie," I said patiently, somehow finding calm in my sister's hysterics, "I can't go to mom's. If the dark magic has taken over the necromancer, it will be stronger than ever. I have to go somewhere it won't find me."

"But where?"

"I shouldn't tell you," I decided. "I can't risk that any spirits might be watching you." And I could only hope none were watching me now, though hopefully Martha would notice. No one could say what manner of spirits the necromancer already had under his control.

"Addy, let us help you."

Martha told me the turn was coming up, so I slowed, searching for the street sign. "Oh you're going to have to help me, and I want you to tell mom everything I just told you. Hopefully one of us can come up with a plan. All I know is I'm not going home until we deal with the necromancer."

"Okay, I guess that's smart, but you better answer your phone the next time I call. I'm going to call mom right now."

At Martha's instruction, I stopped in front of a large white Victorian. "Thanks Callie."

"Don't thank me yet, just be careful. I love you."

"I love you too." I hung up, then picked up Spooky and got out of the car, following Martha as she floated up the driveway.

The house looming over us in the darkness was huge. I could see why Blake was excited about inheriting it.

Martha floated over the grass toward an ornamental shrub. "There's a fake rock at the base of this bush," she explained. "There's a key inside."

I put Spooky down, then got on my knees to search, quickly finding the rock. I used it on the front door, then the three of us went inside and I locked it behind me.

I glanced around at the dark, still interior, not feeling

as safe as I should have, then risked switching on a lamp. No one should be able to find me here, which was both good and bad. Good, because the necromancer probably couldn't find me, but bad, because if he did, there would be no one to come to the rescue.

I walked across the wooden floor of Martha's living room and slumped down onto the sofa. It felt stiff and unfamiliar, and not in the least bit comforting. I sent a quick text to Callie to let her know I was safe for the night.

Spooky hopped up beside me, then nudged my hand with his nose.

I scratched his head. "You saved me tonight."

He started purring. I wished he could speak to me more often, especially now, but I was still grateful he was with me.

Martha floated in front of us. "Try to get some rest. I'll keep watch."

I gave her a small smile. "Thanks, Martha. Thanks for not leaving me behind when the necromancer came. He could have banished you if he wanted."

"Yes, I had a feeling that was the case, but I'm not one to run from a fight, and neither are you. You'll figure out what to do about this necromancer fellow in the morning." She winked at me.

I curled up on the couch, pulling down a throw blanket to put over me, then gathered Spooky up in my arms to keep him warm. I left the lamp on—I just couldn't quite bear to be in full darkness—then closed my eyes.

Sleep came quickly, and I could only hope that it would still be just the three of us hanging out come morning.

CHAPTER NINETEEN

The sound of keys in the lock and masculine voices outside woke me. For just a moment I couldn't remember where I was, then my eyes flew wide.

Martha was crouched right in front of me. "Hurry Addy! Follow me!"

I tossed the blanket off of me, lifted the still sleeping Spooky, then bolted after Martha further into the house. We went through a large kitchen with the first rays of dawn streaming in through a bank of windows, then into an expansive office done up in shades of beige.

Martha stopped in front of an interior door. "In here. It's a closet."

I didn't question her, I could hear the front door opening and the male voices grew louder as they stepped inside. I shut myself in the closet, then put Spooky down by my feet, hoping he knew good enough to stay quiet.

It sounded like both men were wearing loafers,

clacking across the kitchen tiles. I held my breath, pressing my back against one wall, willing them to stay away from the office.

My heart thundered in my ears as their voices grew even closer. They were both in the office!

"I'm sure they're here," one voice said. "Look over there."

Martha appeared in the closet with me, with a few coats bisecting her body. I was glad it was dark, or it would have been unnerving to look at too closely.

"What are Alex and Jackson doing here?" she whispered, though the men couldn't hear her. "What are they looking for?"

I heard desk drawers opening and closing, then one voice said, "They wouldn't fit in there, what are you doing? Check the closet."

My heart fell to my feet. It was a small closet, there was nowhere for me to hide.

I snapped my eyes shut, and thought of a spell. I wasn't powerful enough to actually make myself invisible, but I could will the eye away. As long as both these men were full mundanes and not in the least bit sensitive, they might not see me.

I thought about Spooky too late, but he pushed against my ankle just as the closet door opened.

I opened my eyes just a crack. A man around Martha's age, who I assumed to be Alex, peered inside. He was handsome and clean cut, with a worried crease at his brow. After giving the closet a quick once over, he shut the door.

I nearly slumped to the ground in relief. My magic must have gotten stronger, because I really didn't expect the spell to work. Illusion had never been a strong suit of mine.

The footsteps and voices retreated as they went to search the rest of the house. Martha left me, presumably to follow them.

Eventually I did slump down to sit. It felt like I had been in the closet for over an hour by the time they finally left. Spooky had fallen asleep beside me, seemingly none too worried about any of it.

Even after I heard the front door open and shut, I stayed put, waiting for Martha to return and tell me the coast was clear.

When she finally returned, she was crying. She huddled in the closet with me, wiping tears that would never fall off her face, since they were as incorporeal as she was. "I think they were searching for the paintings that Cheryl took. They both must have known about them. I don't understand. Alex isn't a criminal."

I didn't argue with her, though all signs pointed to Alex not being exactly who she thought he was. Both her ex husband and her employee knew about the stolen paintings, and they wanted them back. I couldn't help but wonder if they were valuable enough to kill over. If either of them thought Martha was onto them, would they kill to cover it up? It was the most plausible motive we had found so far, though I couldn't bring myself to say it out loud.

I stood and waited with Martha while she processed what was going on. When she hadn't spoken for a while, I opened the door and staggered stiff-legged out of the closet. My phone buzzed in my pocket, and I suddenly realized how lucky I was that it hadn't gone off while Alex and Jackson were in the office.

I saw Luna's name on the caller ID and answered it.

"Thank goddess you answered," she sighed. "It seems things have escalated."

My gut clenched. "What do you mean?"

"Mom sensed the dark magic at her house last night. She stayed inside her wards, and luckily it didn't try to break through because she's not sure she could have kept it out. I just got to your house and the place has been ransacked. You were right to not come home."

My knees buckled, and I slumped to the floor. "Ransacked?"

"I think the necromancer was trying to figure out where you went. We finally got a hold of Logan and he's coming over. Apparently mom had asked him to keep you out of the murder investigation because you had more than enough to deal with. He thought he was doing you a favor in ignoring everyone's calls, until I left him a message saying you were in danger."

I rubbed my forehead, feeling dizzy. "We should have let him continue ignoring us. This is too dangerous to involve him in."

"The necromancer is human. If all else fails, maybe he can be arrested."

"If he doesn't kill everyone first!"

She was silent for a moment. "He really has you scared, doesn't he?"

"You bet he does, and now I'm worried for the rest of you. We all should be hiding out, not just me."

Another moment of silence. "We can't all just hide. We have to deal with this. Mom called in cousin Amber."

"Seriously?" I balked. Amber was actually my mom's cousin, not ours. I guess that made her a second cousin? Or maybe distant aunt? I wasn't sure, but I did know mom hated cousin Amber. She wouldn't call her if things weren't dire. "Then I'll come back home. We're stronger together."

"You're the one he wants, Addy. Let the rest of us deal with this. Can you stay where you're hiding today?"

I watched Martha as she floated near the window, peering outside, her gaze distant. "I think so, but Luna, how are we going to deal with this?"

"Amber is as strong as mom, maybe stronger. We'll figure it out, Addy. We'll keep you safe. I need to go, I think Logan is here."

I winced. I really didn't want Logan getting involved in this. "Let him look around, file a report, then get him out of there and don't call him again."

"Okay, sis. Be safe." She hung up.

Just as I lowered my phone, it buzzed again. Logan's name popped up on the caller ID, but I ignored it. He would have a lot of questions, and I wouldn't have any answers.

Martha turned to me. "Addy, I know you're going through a lot right now, but we need to figure out why Alex was here looking for those paintings. If they think I took them, one of them might have killed me."

"But how are we supposed to figure that out?"

She frowned, apparently as at a loss as I was.

Remembering something from the previous night, I removed the slip of paper Spooky had found at Cheryl's from my back pocket. I punched the address into my phone, my eyes widening at what popped up. A pawn-shop in the city. Maybe the one where Cheryl had abandoned the stolen paintings?

I stared down at the address. It was only about a thirty minute drive, and I wouldn't mind a distraction from worrying about what my family was dealing with without me.

"Martha," I said, looking up at her, "I think I have an idea."

Hope sparkled in her eyes, and I prayed I wasn't just leading her to a dead end. It was a long-shot, but if I could get my hands on those stolen paintings, I might be able to use them to get Alex or Jackson to tell me the truth.

I might not be strong enough to deal with a possessed necromancer, but maybe I could at least bring one friendly ghost her justice.

CHAPTER TWENTY

I sipped the last of my to go cup of coffee as we pulled up to the small parking lot of the pawnshop. I had felt a little weird about going through Martha's pantry and using her coffee pot, but she had insisted I have breakfast. It just seemed wrong to eat her food and use her things in front of her when she would never be able to use them again. I felt a little less guilty about the can of tuna I'd found for Spooky, but only a little.

Martha leaned over in the back seat, peering through the window at the pawnshop. "I can hardly picture Cheryl coming to a place like this."

I observed the building with her, and I had to agree. Cheryl, who had bawled her eyes out about stealing stolen paintings, had walked past these barred up windows with hopes of fast cash and an end to her troubles. "Why wouldn't she just sell the cabin?" I muttered to myself.

"Well, she's very proud of it," Martha answered. "I do wonder where her money troubles came from to begin with though. The cabin was left to her free and clear, and she has worked at the bank for years."

I shrugged, not really thinking much of it. People found all sorts of ways to get themselves into debt, even when they made enough to live on without it.

I glanced at Spooky, debating leaving him in the car, then thought better of it. I suspected his presence had given me the extra power to hide myself when Alex looked in the closet, maybe he could help me charm whoever ran the pawnshop.

I unbuckled my seatbelt, then looked to Martha. "Maybe you can snoop around while I ask about the paintings. If the guy knew they were stolen, he might not be keen on answering any questions."

With a nod, Martha popped out of sight.

I grabbed Spooky and walked across the lot toward the pawnshop, tuning out the din of traffic and distant voices that was the constant soundtrack of the city, even a small city like Wickenburg. I wasn't sure how people could live in places like this where there were hardly any trees and silence was a thing found only with earplugs.

I reached the door and went inside, taking a quick look around. The shop was five times the size of Blake's place and ranged from expensive furniture and electronics, to jewelry and leather coats. Near the counter were power tools and more expensive electronics like video game consoles, along with diamond rings beneath a glass display case. Behind the counter stood an older man with thinning gray hair and a round belly. Hopefully he was the same guy Cheryl had talked to. There was a door at his back, either leading to an office or storage. Or maybe it was just a bathroom and nothing interesting at all.

He gave me a wary smile, glancing at the black cat on my right arm, but not making comment. I imagined he saw all sorts in a shop like this.

"Can I help you?" he asked as I reached the counter.

I gave him a friendly smile. "I'm a buyer of antiques, I'm wondering if you have any *special* pieces to offer."

His smile faltered. "Everything I have is out on the floor, feel free to take a look."

I stepped a little closer, glancing to make sure no other customers were nearby. "Are you sure? I'll pay good money for *rare* pieces."

His eyes narrowed. "What sort of *rare* pieces?"

"Oh anything, but primarily paintings."

He splayed his fingers on the glass countertop. "Look lady, if you're a cop, you're barking up the wrong tree. I'm not doing anything illegal here, and I haven't done anything to deserve being hassled."

Martha melted through the door at his back, an excited grin on her face. She pointed to the back room and mouthed, *Paintings.*

I gave her a subtle nod and smiled charmingly at the man in front of me. I was only going to have one shot at this, so hopefully I didn't blow it. "I assure you, sir, I'm not a cop, but I do know one. He would probably be pretty interested in the paintings you have stashed in that room behind you. Do yourself a favor and leave them in the back alleyway and I'll take care of the problem for you."

His skin turned paler than Martha floating next to him. "Look, some lady just left them here. I don't want any problems."

"Like I said, leave them out back and I'll take care of it. No one has to know."

His sagging cheeks puffed as he let out a long breath. "Fine, just get rid of them. I should've thrown them in the dumpster to begin with."

I didn't ask him why he hadn't. If they were valuable enough to steal, they were valuable enough to sell if you knew the right people. Since I didn't care about selling them, I didn't bother to ask.

I gave him a little salute with my free hand, then walked confidently back out of the store, hoping he wasn't trying to trick me.

After waiting a few minutes in the car, we drove around back and sure enough, the paintings were there wedged behind a dumpster. There were five of them, and fortunately they weren't too big to fit into my trunk. I didn't really want to be caught driving around with stolen paintings in the back seat.

Once they were secure, we headed back toward Martha's.

"So what's our next step?" she said excitedly, leaning forward near my shoulder.

I took a turn that would lead us out onto the highway. "We'll send each of the men a text with a picture of some of the paintings, and we'll offer them a deal. They tell us who killed you, and we give the paintings back, no questions asked. They obviously want them pretty badly."

"But what if they each say the other one did it?"

I hadn't really thought about that. "Then we ask them for proof. And even if they don't have it, if they each accuse each other then we know that one of them is probably the killer."

"I suppose it's a start," Martha sighed. "I just hope I don't run out of time. I want to be around long enough to help you with your problem too."

I smiled, glad I made the choice to help Martha today instead of worrying about my own problems. I mean, I was still worried about them, and worried about my family, but it felt like there was nothing I could do on that end. At least if I helped Martha, I wouldn't be totally useless.

"So say we actually figure out who the murderer is," Martha pondered. "How are we going to prove it?"

I frowned, keeping my eyes on the road. "That's going to have to be a problem for another day. If I tell Logan I know who the killer is, I think he'll believe me. Then at least he'll know right where to look for proof."

"You would trust the same man who ignored your calls all day yesterday?"

I sighed, unable to come up with a good answer. I understood why he had ignored my calls, he was trying to keep me out of trouble. I understood it because today, I would be doing the same to him.

CHAPTER TWENTY-ONE

Once we were back at Martha's house I spread the paintings out on a white sheet in her office and started taking
pictures with my phone. I didn't want the flooring to give
away where the paintings were, and now that Martha's
house had already been searched, it should be the last
place either of them would look.

I had talked to Luna on the drive back. Logan filed a
report on the break in, and wanted to know where I was.
I was starting to feel bad about ignoring his calls, but I
wasn't sure what I could tell him. I definitely didn't want
him out looking for the necromancer, but to prevent that
I would have to lie to him. I wasn't sure why, but I didn't
want to lie.

And so, he got ignored, and I would solve the case
without him.

Once I had enough pictures on my phone, I turned
to Martha. "I was thinking about how I would contact

them. If I send a text, they might be able to look me up by my number, but if I create a fake email they won't know who it's coming from. Maybe someone tech savvy enough could trace the IP address, but that would take time."

She turned toward her desk and reached for a drawer, her hand going right through it. "Oh my, why did I think that would work?" she muttered.

I stepped around and opened the drawer for her, giving her a wary glance.

"My address book," she explained pointing downward. "I have Jackson's email in there. Alex's I know by heart." She reached for the address book and her hand passed through, as if she had already forgotten again that she couldn't physically touch things. She looked at her hand like it had betrayed her.

I gingerly picked up the address book, still watching her closely. "Are you all right?"

She scratched her transparent nose, looking at the book in my hands. "I just feel a bit fuzzy and tired. This is the first time I've felt tired since I died."

She was continuing to fade, and I wasn't sure if telling her as much would make it better or worse. "Why don't you rest a little while? I'll send the emails to Alex and Jackson. I'll let you know when they reply."

She nodded, her eyes distant, then she floated out of the room. Spooky watched her float away, then trotted after her.

"All right, Jackson," I muttered as I sat crosslegged on the floor. "You first."

I found his email easily enough, and Alex's since Martha had forgotten to give it to me. I made a fake email on my phone to send from, linking it to my mail app so I would get notifications. Once that was ready I sent them both identical messages, telling them that if they told the other about the email, the paintings would be burned.

Now all that was left to do was wait. I hid the paintings in the office closet, throwing the sheet then some coats over them. Hopefully Blake wouldn't come by to start appraising the house. He would probably recognize the paintings Cheryl had tried to sell him and might mention to Alex that they were here.

I had just closed the closet door when my phone buzzed. I pulled it out of my pocket to see a new email, a reply from Alex.

All it said was, "Meet me tonight, 9 PM," followed by an address.

I hurried out of the office to show Martha and ask her if she knew the address, but found her hovering horizontally over the couch, her eyes closed.

Spooky was sitting on an adjacent chair watching her.

I sidled up to him. "I think all this flitting around wore her out," I whispered. "We'll let her rest until it's time to meet Alex."

Spooky blinked up at me, then continued watching Martha.

Since I had time to kill, I went into the kitchen and called Luna again, but it was Callie who answered.

"What's up, sis?" she asked. I could hear her boots echoing across flooring as she walked away from other voices.

"Why are you answering Luna's phone?"

She chuckled. "Cousin Amber will be arriving in a few hours. Luna and mom are strategizing on how to handle her."

I sighed. "Well at least she's coming. I'll feel better about leaving the rest of you to face the necromancer with her around."

"Yeah, it's afterward that I'm worried about. Last time I thought we'd never get rid of her. She agrees though that you should stay away. The dark magic could possess you and use you against us."

I shook my head, though she couldn't see it. "Last time I had to let the dark magic in willingly."

"Well from the sounds of it, the necromancer didn't let it in willingly, but it went for him anyways. And now with his magic, this thing will be stronger than ever. You need to stay put wherever you are." She was silent for a moment. "You *are* staying put, right Addy?"

I had been planning on telling her about my meeting with Alex, but her words made me think better of it. I didn't need my mom or my sisters worrying about me when they had something serious to deal with. "Yeah, I'm staying put. Bored, but perfectly safe."

"Bored and safe is better than possessed or dead," she replied. "Now I better go help strategize."

"All right, be safe."

We hung up and I leaned against the counter. Now I just had to wait for nightfall. And oh yeah, meet with a potential murderer. If Jackson got back to me and accused Alex, I might rethink my plan to not tell anyone where I was going, but for now I'd keep quiet.

I glanced around the kitchen, thinking I might as well make myself some lunch. With a long night ahead, I'd need all the strength I could get.

CHAPTER TWENTY-TWO

When Martha awoke she seemed more muddled than ever. She pretended to know what I was talking about when I mentioned the emails, but I could tell that she was confused. I would have left her behind to preserve what was left of her energy, but I really needed her to catch Alex in a lie, or to otherwise confirm that he wasn't putting me on about anything.

Once we were all in my car and ready to go, I showed her the address, but she didn't recognize it. It wasn't far though, and it was only 8:15. Plenty of time to get there early and scope things out.

"Remind me again why we're going to see Alex," Martha said from the back seat as I started driving.

Almost time, a voice said in my head.

I glanced at Spooky in the passenger seat. *Almost time for what?* I thought. *Time for Martha to move on?*

My thoughts received no reply, though at this point I

hadn't expected one. "We are going to ask him about the stolen paintings," I said out loud. "We're trying to figure out who killed you."

"Oh, I would have liked to not remember that part. I'm not sure I can bear finding out if it's Alex."

I took a left turn, following the GPS on my phone while I gave it a fresh charge with my car charger. I was worried about Martha, but I couldn't stop thinking about my family. It was dark now, cousin Amber would be with them and they would be looking for the necromancer. Could I really let them face him without me? Did I have a choice?

I doubled my attention on the road, pushing away my thoughts. Nothing I could do about any of it right this moment, and Callie was right. The dark magic had tried to use me against mom before, I couldn't let that happen again.

We spent the rest of the drive in silence, save another call from Logan, which I ignored. I slowed as I went around the final turn, pulling up to a fenced lot of storage containers. My gut clenched. It looked like the perfect place to murder someone and hide a body in a freezer, or maybe I just watched too many murder mystery shows.

I didn't see any other vehicles, so I parked in an adjacent lot. I would take a look around, then hide until Alex arrived to make sure he was alone.

Once we were out of the car, Spooky and Martha both followed at my heels as I walked along the chain-link fence, looking for a way in other than the locked gate. This was the address Alex had given me, but he didn't say exactly where we should meet. Maybe he wanted to meet outside of the perimeter, which was fine by me. The dark storage containers gave me the creeps.

After exhausting my search, I crouched in the deeper darkness of a small tree outside the fence. Anyone approaching shouldn't immediately notice me unless they shined a flashlight directly my way.

I tensed at the sound of tires crunching on gravel and the thrum of an engine, then looked over my shoulder. A car approached, its headlights off and its interior bathed in blackness.

I almost fled then and there, but I couldn't lose this opportunity. Martha was quickly running out of time.

I waited in silence until the car door opened, and Alex stepped out. He wore a black turtleneck sweater and black slacks with a matching stocking cap pulled over his gray hair like he was in some bad spy movie. He glanced around, searching for me, though he didn't know it was me he was searching for.

I took a steadying breath. Here went nothing. I hadn't heard anything back from Jackson, and now Alex would be able to ID me. This was probably my only chance to figure out what really happened to Martha.

I stood and started walking toward him.

His eyes landed on me across the hood of his car, and I think they widened, though it was hard to tell with clouds concealing the moon.

I reached his car, then stayed on the other side of the

hood. "I'm here, now tell me whatever you couldn't say over an email."

He blinked at me. "Who are you?"

"That doesn't matter," I said. "Tell me what happened to Martha, and I'll give you back the paintings."

His breath fogged the night air. "I think Jackson killed her, but I can't prove it. At least if I have the paintings to turn in, I can send the cops in the right direction."

Even though I was halfway expecting the accusation, it felt like my breath had been sucked out of me. Either I was finally about to find out why Martha was killed, or she could help me realize that Alex was actually the killer and was lying to me.

"Why do you think he killed her?" I asked.

He rubbed his eyes, which made me look a bit closer at him. His skin was sallow and his face drooped. Before me was a man who wasn't getting much sleep.

"I think he killed her because of the paintings," he explained. "Or maybe because of the gallery. I had been suspicious for a while, so I started looking up the artwork he was bringing in."

"Was it stolen?"

"No, it was all above board, but I noticed something else that was strange. There were more empty delivery crates than there were paintings, but these extra paintings were nowhere to be found. I think he usually moved them out quickly, but one day I saw them before he could and I looked them up. They were stolen. I was ready to turn him in to the police then and there, but when I went back the paintings were gone."

Cheryl, I thought. That must've been the day Cheryl went to the gallery and stole the paintings. "Were they valuable?" I asked.

He nodded. "Exceedingly so. Jackson had been trying to convince me to sell him the gallery for months, but half of it belonged to Martha, so even if I was ready to sell I wasn't about to force the issue. I think he was going to use the sale of the paintings to buy me off."

I shook my head. "So did he kill Martha because he thought she took the paintings, or because he wanted her out of the way so he could buy the gallery?"

"I don't know," he breathed. "Maybe both."

Martha popped up beside me, making me jump because I had almost forgotten she was there. "Ask him why he was helping Jackson look for the paintings in my house." Her eyes were steady and sure, not a hint of the confusion showing from earlier. Being around Alex must have revived her memories.

I asked her question.

Alex gasped. "How do you know about that?"

"I'm the one asking the questions. Why were you searching Martha's house with the man you think killed her?"

His shoulders slumped. "Jackson claimed he and Martha were working together to import some rather valuable paintings. He wanted to sell them in order to buy the gallery from me. It was clearly a lie, I had seen the stolen paintings and they had nothing to do with Martha. But the fact that he thought she might have them—" He shook his head. "I knew that the paintings were stolen, but he doesn't know that I know. I put two and two together. Only Martha, Jackson, and I have access to the gallery. I didn't take them, so Martha must have, and maybe that's why he killed her. I thought that if I pretended to believe him I could get more evidence, or I could maybe even get the paintings to turn in to the police."

I couldn't exactly ask Martha if she believed what he was saying, but it was clear by her expression that she did. She gazed at him with love, her ex-husband who even though he wasn't romantically in love with her, still loved her enough to want to bring her justice.

"One last question," I said. "Why was there a contract to sell the gallery on your desk?"

He stared at me. "How do you know all of this?" He held up his hand. "Never mind, I don't want to know. Jackson had that contract drawn up months ago. He knew I wanted to sell, and Martha didn't. He thought maybe if there was a contract for her to look over with a monetary offer she might be swayed. When I discovered how much the paintings were worth, I pulled out the contract to compare the amount Jackson was offering for the gallery."

I took a deep breath. It all made sense. "I'll bring the paintings to the police and point them in Jackson's direction. I hold a small amount of sway with the homicide department."

Alex's eyes lit up. "You mean you'll back up my story?"

I nodded.

He exhaled loudly. "This is such a relief. You don't know what this means to me. Who are you?"

I smiled. "I'm a friend of Martha's, that's all you need to know."

He nodded, laughing nervously. "I suppose that is an answer I will have to accept. You know how to contact me. Please let me know when it is done."

I inclined my head.

With a final long look at me, he got in his car and drove off.

Martha floated beside me, watching him go. "Alex didn't kill me. It was Jackson. And he's going down."

I really hoped he would indeed go down, though I still needed to convince Logan. "Let's go get the paintings and bring them to the police."

Spooky meowed, and I heard a click behind me.

I turned to find a young man with gelled blonde hair and dark sinister eyes pointing a gun at me.

I raised my hands and swallowed the lump in my throat. "Jackson, I presume?"

"You presume correctly. Give me your phone."

My hand was surprisingly steady as I lowered it to my pocket. I pressed the screen unlock button, then tapped what I hoped was the call button twice.

I withdrew the phone and handed it to him. "How did you find me?" I asked, hoping to cover the sound of the phone calling back my most recent call.

Jackson didn't seem to notice, and just shoved the phone in his jacket pocket. "We all share the same computer at work, and Alex hasn't changed his email password in years."

Darn, maybe I should have sent texts after all. I kept my hands raised as he aimed the gun at my head. "What do you want from me?" I rasped.

"I want you to take me to my paintings."

I glanced at Martha, almost wishing she were a more powerful scary spirit. No magic I had was going to stop a bullet. And once Jackson had his paintings, he had no reason to keep me alive.

CHAPTER TWENTY-THREE

Jackson sat in the front passenger seat with the gun aimed in my general direction as I pulled my car away from the storage lot. He hadn't seemed to notice Spooky hopping in right ahead of him before darting onto the floor of the back seat, he was too busy pointing his gun at me. Martha had disappeared. I didn't know where she went. Maybe she had faded away entirely.

"I told you the paintings are at Martha's, in the office closet," I repeated. "There's no need to bring me with you."

He brandished his weapon. "Oh no, we are going to make sure they're there. You've already caused enough issues with Alex. I can't buy the gallery now, but I can still sell the paintings. Once they're gone, there will be no proof against me."

I gripped the steering wheel tightly and took the next turn, hoping Logan was listening in through my phone, or at least getting a voicemail. "So did you kill Martha for the paintings, or for the gallery?"

He laughed. "I honestly thought Alex was the one who took the paintings. I thought I could get rid of Martha, then use the stolen paintings to blackmail Alex into selling me the gallery. They were stolen after all, and in his possession. But then it became clear to me that he didn't know anything about the paintings—at least that's what I thought. So I told him Martha and I were working together on some imports so I could search her house."

I took another turn. "Then you would sell the paintings and buy the gallery, but why did you need this particular gallery so badly? You could have just sold the paintings and bought some other gallery."

He huffed. "I did all the work of building the gallery to be what it was. I dedicated countless years of my life to that place, but Martha wouldn't even hear of making me a third partner."

I heard a faint beep, and he whipped his eyes to me. "What was that?" He pulled my phone out of his jacket pocket, finally noticing the lit up screen. With a hiss of rage he rolled down the window and threw the phone outside, then turned and pressed the gun to my head. "Drive faster."

Wind buffeted us from the open window. I bit back tears and pushed my foot down on the gas. Logan was my last missed call. If I had managed to leave a voicemail, it would be on his phone. He would know we were going to Martha's, but there was no saying when he would listen to the message. I might be dead by then.

Jackson didn't divulge any more information on the rest of the drive. I slowed the car as we pulled up to Martha's.

"I imagine you have a key," Jackson said as I shut off the engine. "You get out of the car first. Run and I'll shoot you. Once I have the paintings, I'll let you go."

I didn't believe his promise for a second, but there was nothing I could do but obey. I opened my door and got out, leaving it open so Spooky could slink out while Jackson wasn't looking. He got out of the car after me, then kept the gun pointed at my back as I approached the front door. I put the key in the lock. It was too late for any neighbors to be out and about, and too dark for anyone to notice what was happening regardless. I could scream, but he might shoot me and run.

I turned the key, but the door was already unlocked. Odd, I was sure I had locked it. Not saying anything, I opened the door and went inside.

Magic prickled up and down my arms as I stepped across the threshold. "Oh you have got to be kidding me," I groaned.

I felt the gun barrel push against my back. "What? Kidding about what?" Jackson shoved me further into the entry room, swinging the door shut behind us. "Where are the paintings?"

"Back in the office." I pointed, glancing around the deep shadows of the sitting room. The dark magic was

SARA CHRISTENE

here, I could feel it. It had managed to track me down, or maybe the necromancer tracked Martha. And even worse, Spooky had been shut outside.

Jackson gripped my left arm and kept the gun pressed against my back as he shoved me forward. "Show me."

I staggered further into the house, praying I wouldn't trip and cause him to fire the gun. The feel of dark magic grew stronger as I entered the office.

Jackson let me go. "Open the closet door and pull out the paintings."

I stepped forward, knowing the gun would be trained on my back the entire way.

"That is my witch, mortal," a voice I recognized said from behind us.

I turned to see Jackson whirling around, aiming his gun at the necromancer.

The necromancer's hands glowed green with magic. It was the dark magic speaking, not him.

"Y-you better get out of here now!" Jackson's voice broke in fear. I wasn't sure if he could see the magic, or just sensed that the one standing before him was a predator.

The necromancer waved his hand, and Jackson fell to the floor. His gun went skidding under the desk.

I moved away until my back was pressed against the closet door. A hint of moonlight streaming in through the window lit the sickly sweat on the necro-mancer's forehead. He was struggling, fighting against

170

the dark magic, but he wasn't strong enough. None of us were.

He reached one glowing hand out toward me. "Come with me willingly, witch, and I won't have to possess you."

I shook my head, pressing my back against the door as hard as I could. "No thanks, I'll just stay here."

He stepped toward me. The necromancer was at least five inches taller than me. Even without the help of magic, he could probably overpower me.

I shut my eyes and started chanting a protection spell in my head, already knowing it wouldn't be strong enough.

The necromancer's hand clamped down on my shoulder, and my senses were overwhelmed with dark magic. My weak protection spell dissipated.

"Addy!" Martha screamed.

My eyes flew open as Martha streamed into the room, her scream echoed by the front door slamming open on the other side of the house.

"Addy!" Luna's voice called out.

"Adelaide!" My mom echoed her.

"Accursed witches!" the necromancer growled.

Green glowing magic flowed out of his mouth, spewing toward my face. It pushed against my lips, trying to seep through every opening, even my pores.

I sensed the movement of my family pouring into the room, then Spooky pressed against my leg. He must have come inside with them. Martha must have led them here.

My familiar's presence granted me the strength to fight the dark magic. I pictured a ward in my mind, keeping it out.

A moment later, Logan's voice, "Everybody freeze!"

My mom and sisters' voices came together in an ancient chant, and I thought I recognized cousin Amber's voice joining in too, but I couldn't see past the green glow trying to force its way past my shields. My body didn't seem to want to move, and the necromancer's hand still tightly gripped my shoulder.

I could feel the dark magic's rage at the powerful witch's chant. Alone, one witch might not be that strong, but few could stand against an entire coven.

My lips started moving, joining in with the chant.

The necromancer cried out, falling to his knees as the green magic spilled fully out of his mouth and nose, then wafted up toward the ceiling.

I could finally see clearly, or as clear as I could see in the moonlit darkness. My mom, sisters, and Amber all huddled near the door, hands linked together. Martha floated near Logan, who had a gun pointed at the necromancer. Jackson was still unconscious on the floor.

My family finished their chant, and the dark magic fled.

"What the hell!" the necromancer panted. "Where am I?"

I let out a shaky laugh. "I told you that you weren't strong enough to contain the dark magic."

Logan sidled toward me, his gun still pointed at the

necromancer. "Is this the guy who broke into your house?"

I nodded. "I assume you got the voicemail?"

"I heard everything," he confirmed. "Jackson will go down for Martha's murder." He removed a set of handcuffs from his belt, then looked down at the necromancer still on his knees and started reading him his rights.

The necromancer glared at me all the while.

Logan had to call in back up to take both the necromancer and Jackson, then stayed behind with me and my family once they had both been carted off.

I knew I had some serious 'splainin to do, but first there was Martha. She was beginning to lose her form. It was time to say goodbye.

CHAPTER TWENTY-FOUR

We all gathered in Martha's sitting room as she hovered in a seated position above the sofa. She had grown more transparent, her body seeming to lose shape at the edges. Callie had turned on the lights, and now stood back with the rest of my family and Logan.

Martha patted the seat on the sofa beside her, her hand going through the cushion and not actually making a sound.

I sat next to her, turning my body in her direction.

She smiled. "I want to thank you for bringing me peace, Addy. Without you, I never would have known why I was killed, and my killer might not have ever been brought to justice."

I glanced at my family and Logan, feeling awkward taking the praise in front of them. Even Spooky stood off to one side, watching me.

I shrugged and turned back to Martha. "It was Alex

too. If he wouldn't have told me what happened, we might not have figured anything out."

"It was your plan with the paintings. You figured out more than anyone else could."

I was glad Logan couldn't hear her half of the conversation or he might be a little offended. I patted the air near her hand, careful to not let my fingers sink through hers. All I felt was an electric chill, nothing substantial. "Well regardless, I'm glad you're at peace. And I'm glad I got to know you." I glanced at the others again, then back to her. "And thanks for bringing my family here. That was quick thinking on your part."

She let out an audible breath and shook her head. "I felt awful leaving you with that gun-wielding maniac, but I knew you could handle yourself." Her gaze went distant as her eyes tilted up to the ceiling. "I think it's time. Please find a way to thank Alex for me. He doesn't believe in ghosts. I didn't either, but I want him to know I appreciate all he did."

"I'll do my best," I said, but I didn't think that she heard me. Her form dissipated into white mist, then suddenly dispersed.

I turned to the others in the room, finding Logan staring at me wide-eyed. "Did she just . . . depart?" he asked. "I felt it. Like a big pressure shift in the room."

I smiled. "Maybe you're a bit sensitive after all."

He shook his head in disbelief. "I'm going to need someone to explain everything that happened here tonight, and why I had to lie to my officers to cover certain things up."

Cousin Amber stepped forward from the rest. She was tall and thin like my mom, but her hair was jet black, cut into a chin length bob. "First we need to talk about the dark magic. It may have left the necromancer, but it will find someone else."

"And just who was the necromancer?" Callie asked. "Where did he come from?"

"We'll find that out soon," Logan answered. "But I can't guarantee we'll be able to hold him for long. All we have on him is an accusation of breaking and entry, and damaging property. If we don't find anything substantial to tie him to the crime, he'll walk free."

I slumped back against the sofa cushions. It was no use telling Logan what the necromancer had done in the woods. There was no proof of it.

Cousin Amber walked across the room to take a seat next to me, swishing her black skirts. Her nearness brought a thrum of magic. She patted my hand atop my leg. "Don't you worry, Adelaide. We'll figure out what to do about the necromancer, if anything needs to be done at all. After being possessed by the dark magic, he may run for the hills."

I nodded along with her words. "You're right. We'll wait and see what he does."

"We should get going," Logan interrupted, his eyes on me. "Do you mind if I give you a ride home?"

I was too tired to argue. I hugged my mom and sisters

goodbye, received a pat on the head from cousin Amber, then lifted Spooky into my arms. I took one last glance around Martha's home, realizing I was going to miss her. I wasn't sure what I would do to send her thanks to Alex, but I would figure it out.

"Ready?" Logan asked.

I nodded, then we all filed out the front door. The key was still in the lock where I'd left it, and I figured it might as well stay there. It was a nice neighborhood. Things should be fine until Blake could come by and start cleaning things out.

I hardly paid attention as my mom, sisters, and Amber all piled into my mom's truck. I sat in Logan's front passenger seat with Spooky on my lap. As soon as Logan got in and started the engine, he blasted the heat.

I swallowed the lump in my throat. I was safe, for now, and lucky to be alive. Somehow the gun wielding-maniac had scared me more than the dark magic, maybe because I understood magic. I didn't understand killing for money or for an art gallery.

Logan pulled out onto the street, following behind my mom's truck.

I noticed him glancing at me and frowned. "Please don't make me explain everything."

"So the dark magic that had empowered Neil Howard's ghost," he began, "and possessed you in the forest after Ike chased you, came back and possessed the man who broke into your house. That man is also a necromancer, which I assume means he can control the dead. Both the dark magic and necromancer were drawn to you because you are a channelling witch, and they hope to use you in some manner. Did I miss anything?"

I shook my head and let out a weak laugh. "No, I don't suppose you did."

"And you solved Martha's murder."

I stroked Spooky's warm fur. "It was a joint effort. If Spooky wouldn't have stolen a piece of paper from Cheryl's house, I would have never found the paintings. What will happen to them now, by the way?"

He shrugged. "When they're no longer needed as evidence, they'll be returned to their rightful owners."

"So it's over then. Case closed."

He pulled the car out onto the highway. "Well except for the dark magic and glowing animals."

"The necromancer was just using the glowing animals to test if I could really channel. With him no longer keeping the spirits here, they should fade."

"So just the dark magic then," he said.

"Yep."

I peered out the dark window, wondering where the magic had gone. Would it be afraid of us now that cousin Amber was around? Five witches made a full coven. Few things in the supernatural world would mess with a full coven, but I had a feeling the dark magic was an exception. According to the necromancer, it was something long dead, but that's all we really knew about it. But why had something long dead appeared so suddenly?

It was always here, a voice said in my mind. *Waiting for you to be ready.*

I whipped my eyes down to Spooky and almost asked him to repeat what he had just said, then I remembered I was in the car with Logan.

I kept my attention on the cat, meeting his yellow eyes staring back at me. *Why is it I can only hear you on occasion?* I thought.

Because you need to learn to listen. You hear me now because your mind is exhausted.

I frowned. Here I had been blaming the cat for his lack of communication, when it turned out I was just a bad listener.

Story of my life.

CHAPTER TWENTY-FIVE

"Are you sure you're not a zombie?" Richie asked, giving me a speculative look.

I rolled my eyes at him as I steamed milk for a customer's order. He had come in for another day of training, and I had to admit I was grateful. After the last few days, I felt like crap. I needed time off.

"You shouldn't speak to your boss like that," I chided.

He was looking out toward the front, then turned toward me with a grin. "So I also shouldn't give my boss a hard time about her *boyfriend* visiting her."

I glanced toward the door to watch Max come in, then turned a quick glare in Richie's direction. "Not my boyfriend," I hissed under my breath. "Now make him a coffee."

I walked around the counter to greet Max. Spooky watched my progress from the top of his bookshelf. He hadn't spoken to me since the previous night, and I wondered if it really was my fault I couldn't hear him. That I just wasn't listening right.

I met Max at one of the tables near the front window and we both sat. "Don't worry about going up to order," I explained. "Richie has you covered."

Max smiled and raked his fingers through his tousled hair. "Thanks. So he's officially hired?"

I wasn't sure how he always looked so good after touching his hair like that. If I did that to mine I would end up a poof ball. "Officially hired. With all the baking I'm doing, I need to cut back on my hours." *And with all of the witching I've been doing,* I added internally.

"Does that mean I won't see you around here as much?"

I leaned back in my seat and crossed my legs. "Oh I'm sure I will still be here plenty."

Richie came toward our table with two coffees in hand, sliding one in front of each of us. "Why don't you take a break, boss," he said mischievously. "I've got things covered."

Richie turned away as Sophie Eddings came in. Her face lit up when she saw him, though her timid air remained. I made a mental note to return Richie's teasing later, but not in front of Sophie.

I took a sip of my latte, smiling as I realized Richie had sprinkled cinnamon in it, then turned back to Max. "Now where were we, you were lamenting on not seeing me enough?"

I caught him mid-sip and he sputtered on his coffee.

He put down his cup and laughed. "Yeah, I guess that was my point, and I can only see one solution."

I raised a brow. "Go on."

"Let me take you out to dinner this weekend."

I opened my mouth to say yes, then turned as the front door opened and Logan walked in. His expression was dark, and I found myself suddenly dreading whatever he had to say.

He walked toward our table, gave a brief nod of acknowledgment to Max, then looked down at me. "Can I talk to you for a minute?"

"I'll be right back," I said to Max, then stood with my coffee in hand and followed Logan back toward the office.

Sophie and Richie watched on curiously as Spooky hopped off the bookshelf and joined us.

Once we were alone in the office, Logan crossed his arms and shook his head. "You're not going to like what I have to say."

I slumped down into the chair behind my desk. "Just say it."

"My officers lost the necromancer last night. We didn't even have him long enough to ID him."

My jaw fell open. "How did he get away?"

He shrugged. "No one has an explanation for it. He was in the back of a squad car, but when they arrived at the station he was just gone."

I pinched my brow and shook my head. "He probably has illusion magic, I can't believe I didn't realize it before. When I chased him in the woods it was like he was a marathon runner, but it was just an illusion. He had probably circled back around and left me chasing shadows."

"You chased him in the woods?"

I winced. "Yeah, I guess I forgot to mention that."

He sat down on the edge of my desk, angling his body toward me. Spooky jumped up and started sniffing his coat sleeve.

Logan absentmindedly pet the cat. "Do you have any idea who he really was, or where he went?"

I shook my head. "No, and now we may never find out. With cousin Amber around, he would be a fool to approach any of us."

"But are you sure that he won't?"

I thought about it. "No, I'm not sure. True illusion is high-level magic. He might be stronger than we think, though if that's the case, he should have been able to fight off the dark magic."

Logan stared at me, digesting my words. "I'm not going to pretend that half of that isn't beyond my comprehension, but you just let me know if you see him."

I gave him a little salute. "Sure thing, as long as you'll come arrest him and not lose him this time."

He frowned. "And you let me know if the dark magic comes back too."

"You can't arrest dark magic."

He let out a heavy sigh. "Just let me know, please."

"Okay," I agreed, crossing my fingers under the desk.

I might let Logan try to arrest the necromancer again, but I definitely didn't want him anywhere near the dark magic. "How are things going with Jackson?"

"He admitted everything, probably hoping to lessen his sentence."

The stiffness in my shoulders relaxed. I might not have solved anything with the dark magic, but at least Martha's case was closed.

Logan stood and moved toward the door. "You be safe, Addy. Call me if you need anything."

I gave him a wave, then put my head down on the desk as he left and shut the door behind him.

The necromancer will return, Spooky chimed into my mind.

I jolted upright, blinking at the cat on my desk, but he didn't speak further.

I shook my head. I guess he didn't need to. I'd just have to keep the necromancer on my list of worries.

One, dark magic. Two, necromancer. Three, being a channeling witch who naturally drew these dark things toward me.

I glanced at the office door, realizing there was a number four. I needed to hide all of these things from the man I was potentially dating, and I needed to keep him safe. If I knew what was good for both of us, I would avoid him entirely.

But I didn't want to avoid him. So maybe I was a channeling witch surrounded by darkness, did that mean I didn't deserve love?

I was pretty sure I didn't want to know the answer.

THE NEXT FEW days were uneventful. No one saw any glowing animals, necromancers, or green glowing magic. Amber was going to stick around for a while, and joy of joys, she was staying with me. I supposed I couldn't complain. I did feel safer with her around, and it was better than staying out at my mom's.

I sent Alex a care package of baked goods, letting him know they were from me so he didn't think they were poisoned. I thought of Martha while I prepared them, trying to add magic that would remind Alex of her presence. Hopefully some small part of him would be reminded of her, and he would know how grateful she was.

I heard occasional comments from Spooky, and I vowed to be a better listener. Maybe if I kept practicing he would be able to tell me whatever he knew about the dark magic.

Max and I went on our first real date, and so far so good. I could only hope things remained calm . . . but I sure wasn't betting on it.

The Will of Yggdrasil

Fated

Fallen

Fury

Found

Forged

The Thief's Apprentice Series

Clockwork Alchemist

Clocks and Daggers

Under Clock and Key

The Xoe Meyers Series

Xoe

Accidental Ashes

Broken Beasts

Demon Down

Forgotten Fires

Gone Ghost

Minor Magic

Minor Magics: The Demon Code

Printed in Great Britain
by Amazon

61505856R00112